Jerry P. Schellhammer is now authoring book number three and soon will go for more. He was living in Gooding, Idaho, but circumstances forced him back to Spokane, continuing his craft and hoping this series of future books are successful.

See more of his portfolio: *https://jerryschellhammer.com/*

This book is dedicated to my Loraine Powell, my parents, Spokane Fiction Writers Club and Linda Bond.

Jerry P. Schellhammer

FOUR SEASONS – BOOK ONE

Edge of Darkness

AUSTIN MACAULEY PUBLISHERS
LONDON * CAMBRIDGE * NEW YORK * SHARJAH

Copyright © Jerry P. Schellhammer 2025

All rights reserved. No part of this publication may be reproduced, distributed, or transmitted in any form or by any means, including photocopying, recording, or other electronic or mechanical methods, without the prior written permission of the publisher, except in the case of brief quotations embodied in critical reviews and certain other non-commercial uses permitted by copyright law. For permission requests, write to the publisher.

Any person who commits any unauthorized act in relation to this publication may be liable to criminal prosecution and civil claims for damages.

This is a work of fiction. Names, characters, businesses, places, events, locales, and incidents are either the products of the author's imagination or used in a fictitious manner. Any resemblance to actual persons, living or dead, or actual events is purely coincidental.

Ordering Information
Quantity sales: Special discounts are available on quantity purchases by corporations, associations, and others. For details, contact the publisher at the address below.

Publisher's Cataloging-in-Publication data
Schellhammer, Jerry P.
Four Seasons – Book One

ISBN 9781638298687 (Paperback)
ISBN 9781638298694 (Hardback)
ISBN 9781638298700 (ePub e-book)

Library of Congress Control Number: 2025902829

www.austinmacauley.com/us

First Published 2025
Austin Macauley Publishers LLC
40 Wall Street, 33rd Floor, Suite 3302
New York, NY 10005
USA

mail-usa@austinmacauley.com
+1 (646) 5125767

Spokane Fiction Writers Club.

Independence Day
15 October 2014

Mark felt a sudden jerking from the baited fishing line and he quickly pulled on the fishing rod. He reeled in as the mighty German brown, who had tentatively nibbled upon the worm, now put up a fight for its life. It broke the small lake's surface that a second ago appeared still. Now, the brown speckled fish launched itself at least a foot above the surface. After a moment, the three-pound fish reluctantly came upon the shore, still fighting to release itself from the barbed hook placed firmly in its mouth.

This is the fulfillment to a wonderful life I've led, he said to himself as he grabbed the fish with his bare hands. He pulled the hook from the fish, who struggled in this foreign environment. Mark placed the trout inside his cooler of ice-cold water and closed the lid. He remembered what it took to get here; almost 40 years ago, he had yearned for a better life than the one he struggled with as a blue-collar grunt.

He carried the scars to show to all his suffering and resilience to time. His weathered features, his labored breathing and a painful groan as he moved his stiffening legs to sit on a folding angler's stool, showed in his wisdom a willingness to share with others. He wore bib overalls and worn sneakers, so threadbare and full of holes; that Charlotte, his recently engaged fiancée, threatened to burn them in the refuse pit.

I'll be sixty on January first and am already retired; thanks to the Red Widow.

He saw the steady stream of dust billowing from a vehicle heading toward his property, appearing and disappearing among the stands of pine, fir and lodge pole scattered about the road. *Who's coming up here in such a hurry?* He slowly opened his tackle box, a large affair with many compartments, including the large compartment where he kept his loaded .357 Magnum Smith & Wesson revolver in a leather holster. The one he bought when he became a bounty hunter back in '85. He busied himself with placing another nightcrawler upon a hook and casting the line back out to the center of the lake where he spotted another fish jump just now.

The early dawn light made it hard for Mark to determine the make or model of the vehicle coming closer until a quarter mile from his property line; he could see it was a purple Dodge Challenger. It looked brand new and couldn't think of who the person behind the wheel was, until Mark saw Hector's unmistakable bushy mustache, now graying with age, and his fat face that smiled at seeing his friend sitting by the lake-shore.

Hector got out as soon as he stopped the car abruptly on the loose dirt and gravel, creating a thick dust cloud that burned Mark's eyes. "Hey brother, we got a problem."

Mark tried to recover from the intrusion of dust upon his senses before he responded, "Hector, what problem are 'we' having?"

"I got information that Dylan has stumbled upon some crazy-ass terrorist plot with Che Lopez' son, or stepson, with this group based in Mexico, called JANAS. By the way, here's the car to replace the one I wrecked back in '87."

"You know that we're both too damn old for this shit. That is JONAS, Hector. They are the same group that Nicholas Manovich hired to try to take us out last December. Thanks for the car, though; it's about time."

"This may be your last chance to get all of this finally behind you," Hector pointed out as he helped Mark pick up the tackle box and the cooler that held his bait and two bottles of water. "Plus, I think your best friend's son might be in over his head and may need us old timers to rescue him."

"I doubt that," Mark replied to his partner and friend of twenty-seven years when they went to Todos Santos in Baja California. "You're not going to let this go, are you?"

"Not this time, amigo," Hector replied seriously. "A flight is waiting for us at Missoula Airport. Another agent and Chrystal are waiting for us there. Her name is Brodzinski." Mark reluctantly reeled the line back onto the shore, a wistful expression painted on his weathered face. He helped Mark get into the car as Mark remembered the events that had brought this to a head, and it had all started on that fateful day thirty-seven years ago.

12 April 1977

What is with that truck full of electrical wiring? Mark Marteau asked himself as he stood in a short line waiting, while Old Joe interrogated Kurt Jackson. Mark brought cans for recycling, that his boss, Fat Fred, scavenged at the landfill in Richland, Washington. *If it was me, I'd tell that white trash son of a bitch to go elsewhere. I got things to do and don't have time to be standing in line like this.* Mark stood over six foot five and weighed in at over 240 pounds, which was why Fat Fred kept him around; he could take care of the heavy work required to get the job done. He generally wore a grease-stained sweatshirt with jeans and well-worn boots with leather laces.

Mark saw the pickup truck parked in front loaded with bundles of Romex wiring that appeared never to have been used, which young twenty something year old Kurt with thin goatee beard, gestured to Old Joe was his. *It's obviously stolen; still in the original packaging*, Mark opined as he saw Old Joe question the suspicious acting Jackson with his long stringy black hair that came down just past his ears.

Mark glared at Kurt, who he did not know personally, but heard about from his friend, Dave. *From what he told me, he's a heroin addict who would rob his own mother blind to get himself a fix.* He watched Old Joe sitting on a stool, served the acne-scarred young man behind a glass covered counter that had a collection of various auto parts for sale, inside the cabinet and a notepad with the day's date, 12 April 1977 printed on the top.

"Where you say you got this stuff?" Old Joe asked in a mid-western drawl that belied wisdom and knowing bullshit when he heard it as his brow furrowed deep with doubt. *Old Joe could probably hold his own in any bar fight, though he's pushing past 70. His long, wiry legs appear stiff because he recently had knee surgery and his arthritic hands has problems balling up anymore*, Mark thought.

Old Joe wore a pair of bifocal glasses with thick, black frames, which helped him read people's lies better, and liver-spotted and leathery skin from too much sun in his younger days.

"I said I got them from a housing project in Kennewick yesterday," Kurt replied, his voice raised several octaves showing his impatience and frustration at Old Joe's questions.

A farmer stood in front of Mark as he looked outside briefly, and turned around to face the bigger and taller 22-year-old man, "Tell me young man, what year is that old moving van you got there?" Mark noticed the older man was dressed in bib overalls, white and blue checkered buttoned up shirt with I.H. emblazoned ball cap covering his small brown eyes as he saw wisps of white hair around the cap.

"I believe it's a '56, sir," Mark replied respectfully to the older man with large nose, holding a tractor generator in his left hand.

"Yeah, that's what I'm thinking too. It's a pretty old rig," he said and then he turned around as they both heard the young man yell...

"What the hell, you telling me you're going to call the police?" He asked Old Joe, as Mark could see the back of this guy's neck suddenly turn red with anger.

"Just keep your britches on, young man. It's SOP here. I must make sure this stuff wasn't stolen, unless you're licensed and bonded as a salvager. Are you licensed and bonded?"

"No, I'm not licensed or bonded! But I ain't no thief neither."

"Then, you'll have to be patient and wait while I call the police to see if there are any reports of theft. If not, I'll be happy to pay you."

"You son of a bitch," he yelled with contempt. "I ain't no thief!" The old man didn't hesitate and continued to dial the police from the black rotary phone with five clear buttons and one red button just below the rotary dialer.

"Hello, may I speak with Officer Jones, please. It's Old Joe from Tommy Boy Salvage...What's that? Oh, yes, I'll wait. Mike? How you doing? Oh, no complaints. I have someone here who wants me to buy a bunch of household wiring. Oh, wait I guess he's in some sort of hurry to leave. I guess he must have another appointment."

Mark and the farmer watch the drama unfold as the young man pushed pass them and slammed the door with the sign "Thank you, come back again," printed on the door. He got inside the cab of a '61 Ford pick-up, started it up, peeling out from the parking lot, barely missing a tractor with an empty flatbed trailer parked in front of the salvage yard.

"Yeah, I wrote out his license plate number. Are you ready? It's Washington license number I-0975698. Yup, so there was a report filed of stolen wiring; that's what I thought. He didn't look right. He acted funny, like he was high on dope or something. Alright, I'll talk to you later."

"Well, Old Joe, sounds like you earned your money today," the farmer announced.

"It's all in a day's work, Jack. What have you got there?"

"I got a twenty-pound generator that feels more like a hundred twenty pounds right now."

Mark grabbed the generator from the man's hand and hoisted it onto the counter next to the notepad.

"Careful, Mark," Old Joe warned. "That counter is regular glass; ain't tempered."

Mark landed the generator gently on the counter.

"Thanks son," the farmer graciously saluted him, as Mark noticed his red nose was leaking clear mucus onto his gray mustache.

"Not a problem, sir," Mark replied.

"That will be twenty dollars, Jack."

"Twenty dollars?" He railed in mock protest. "Why, you used to give this shit away."

"Well, if you weren't so damn tight with your money, you'd just go to the tractor dealer and buy their generators," Old Joe debated to the farmer.

"Hell, with that," Jack the farmer howled. "Have you seen what they charge for them? It's highway robbery."

"Just give me your Jackson and get the hell out of here, you tight old geezer," Old Joe good naturedly ribbed his friend of thirty years.

Old Joe gave Jack his receipt and he left the shop saying, "Have a good day, Old Joe."

"Now then, Mark you have some cans that you want to sell me. How's Fat Fred doing these days?"

"As well as can be expected I suppose; if metal prices keep dropping, he may have to close everything," Mark replied as his tone became serious.

"It's a tough economy we're having. I can't say it's anyone's fault though everybody likes to blame the president."

"That's because he's a Democrat and an idiot," Mark spat out at his nemesis.

"Well, that may be true, but this economy is very fickle. There are lots of things that can cause what we're experiencing right now."

Old Joe rung up the price and the old man wrote out a check for fifty dollars. "At twenty-five cents a pound, you had two hundred pounds of cans for a grand total of fifty dollars."

"Fred will be pissed. That's hardly worth wasting fuel on that truck for. And we held on until there was no more room in the sorting shop to store them, just with the hope the price would go up."

"What the hell's going on out there?" Old Joe asked, directing Mark's attention outside of the shop. Mark and Old Joe could see the glint of a .38 revolver reflecting off the mid-morning sun. Kurt returned his face a mask of single purpose. He looked to be alone.

"Mark, go into the office and call the police, there's about to be a murder committed here. Don't just stand there, move!"

Mark took a second to spy his old friend reaching for an ancient double-barrel shotgun, sawed off at barely over eighteen inches, as he watched Old Joe pull both hammers back while he ran into the adjacent office, closed the door and grabbed the phone on the desk. Mark dialed the number on a pad sitting next to the phone. "Yes, I'm Mark Marteau and I'm at Tommy Boy Salvage, and I think there's about to be…" Mark heard the commotion in the other room:

"What the hell do you want now, you son of a bitch?" Followed by, "I ain't leavin' till you give me money for my wire!"

"Who the hell are you?" Two quick shots rang out in the small shop, followed by a more powerful blast that Mark could only assume came from Old Joe's shotgun, followed by an eerie silence. Mark tried to remain calm, but panic and fear began to overwhelm his voice, as it seemed to be more unnaturally high pitched than a moment ago. "Did you hear that? Someone got shot. Get the police here now!"

He hung up the phone abruptly and rushed out of the office, expecting to see the worse. He saw Old Joe lying flat on his back with a pair of bullet wounds on his mid-section as Mark came up close to the dying old man. The other guy was nowhere to be seen. A blood trail led out the shop door to where the pickup he drove in had disappeared. Mark tried to comfort Old Joe as much as possible. "What can I do to help?"

"You go find that bastard and hunt him down like the rabid dog he is and kill him," Old Joe said as his final request before he expired in front of him.

Mark thought it queer, how someone who was alive five seconds ago, would be suddenly dead now. Mark felt stunned at this sudden development. He tried to think, but couldn't, as if his mind suddenly took a momentary vacation. He saw the opened cash drawer and would have never considered it before. He would never consider such a thing, except Fred needed the money desperately. *It's an armed robbery gone bad*; Mark reasoned. *That low life scum deserves to have one more charge brought against him anyway.*

He quickly emptied the cash drawer and stuffed the bundle of cash in his pockets. He quickly glanced at the notepad sitting on the glass counter and saw Old Joe's blood splattered across the date, and then, a moment later, the police arrived.

Mark let them inside after they were certain he wasn't the bad guy while they frisked him for weapons. They asked him the standard questions police normally ask. Then they went to work finding out who killed Old Joe.

"Did you see what happened?" Officer Smith asked Mark, who was still visibly shaking as he looked down at Old Joe's corpse.

"No," Mark replied honestly. "I called you from the office over there. The asshole that done it, had been here before trying to sell a load of house wiring that Joe was suspicious about, and called someone over in Kennewick."

"Do you know who?"

"I never met the man."

"I mean, do you know who he tried to call? Was it a police officer over there?"

"Yeah, but…wait, he had a business card on that Rolodex."

The officer looked on the business card attached to the Rolodex. He dialed the number and he heard the familiar voice of a dispatch officer from Kennewick Police.

"Hey, this is Officer Gene Smith at Pasco Police. Is Officer Jones available? Thank you." He wrote something down on a small black note pad.

"Mike? How is it going? This is Gene Smith over at Pasco. Yeah, I got some bad news to report. Old Joe is dead. The guy he wouldn't buy house wiring from apparently came back and robbed him and then shot him. It looks like there's a good size blood trail here, though. Therefore, I would send someone over to Kennewick General to see if anyone has shown up in the last five minutes. Yeah, at least he didn't go without putting up a fight. Right, it's a twelve-gauge shotgun; sawed off. According to the witness here, the perp shot him first, and then Old Joe nailed him with Betsy. Yeah, just like the Wild West. Okay, I'll talk with you later."

Detective Tracy Dickerson arrived as he asked Mark to step outside. He suddenly felt unsteady for the first time. Mark saw the hearse parked next to the van and another patrol car had conveniently blocked the van, so Mark couldn't leave, as an overwhelming sense of loss gripped his gut and he briefly sobbed and a pair of tears rolled down his cheek. Mark calmed himself down and approached the two officers, who were talking among themselves.

"What can I do for you kid?" The taller of the two asked Mark.

"Kid?" Mark said in disbelief. "I'm hardly that. Um, can I get you to contact my boss Fred at the Richland landfill?" Both officers looked at each other as if they were waiting for the other to volunteer.

"Yeah, sure I'll go ahead and do it," Officer Thompson said. He moved over to his patrol car's passenger seat and called Dispatch. "Yeah, the witness to the 10-72 requests we contact his boss, Fred at the landfill in Richland."

"Copy 11:37," the Dispatch responded.

Detective Dickerson came outside and motioned Mark back inside the shop. His salt and pepper crew cut hairstyle made him look like a Marine drill sergeant, as he looked lean and mean with a very stern and serious face. "I have something I want to show you, Mr. Marteau." Mark followed him into the office, "Sit right here behind the desk."

Mark did as directed, not certain what this was about. Once he sat down though, a lump the size of an ostrich egg formed in his throat when he saw the video recorder and TV monitor on a shelf that had the image of the counter and the cash register.

"Did you know that Old Joe had this new-fangled technology? He wasn't dumb, son. He didn't make it in this part of town without an edge," the detective stated in a direct manner.

Mark didn't say anything as the detective proceeded to press Play and, on the screen, was the shooting, and then the 'robbery.'

"I'm sorry, Mr. Marteau, but I'm not seeing anyone, but you taking the money from the cash register."

Mark continued to keep his mouth shut as he pulled the cash from his pants pockets and placed it on the desk. "I'm sorry; I didn't know anything about this," Mark said referring to the shooting between Old Joe and Kurt Jackson, pointing at the monitor for emphasis. "I was just pissed that we can't seem to get ahead in this business. Fred wanted more than fifty dollars to show for having to work all those hours, picking all those cans."

"I can empathize with you son. But this isn't it. Now you're going to jail for what you did. I wish I could help but I can't."

An idea crossed Mark's mind like an epiphany.

"How about if you could make me be like an informant?" Mark asked in desperation. The detective, under any other circumstances, would have said no. It smacked of vigilantism. But he also didn't want to put this kid in jail for doing something he claimed was honorable or done for the right reason. The detective asked, "Do you know who Kurt Jackson is?"

"Is that his name?" Mark asked.

Dickerson nodded, as Mark replied, "No I don't know who he is."

He very reluctantly said, "On one condition. No weapons, you tell me everything, and once you know one hundred percent where he is, you call me and walk away. You do that, and I'll make sure you get credit for the bust and a substantial cash reward."

Mark knew the old man wanted him to take him out. However, he also knew this detective was offering him a gift; a gift that he would be stupid to say no to. "How much is the reward?"

"It varies. Most cash rewards for murder are between twenty-five and fifty thousand. I bet that's more money than you've ever seen in your life. Isn't it?"

Mark could only nod. "Yeah, I'll agree to your terms. Old Joe will have to see that bastard go to hell some other way."

The images kept playing over and over in his head as he drove the two-ton moving van out to the landfill. The landfill sat off state route 240 about four miles outside Richland. *Damn my luck that Old Joe had a security camera there,* Mark thought. *What the hell was I thinking?* The large cumbersome truck moved slowly up the winding one percent grade as elevation slowly climbed to over 800 feet from 600 feet at the town of Richland.

Cars passed him easily as they drove the maximum speed limit of the posted 55 miles per hour; the van, on a good day, could barely go pass 45 miles per hour. Rattlesnake Ridge stood imposing in front of him as he drove increasingly closer to the largest bald-face ridge in North America.

He down shifted the truck and turned onto the landfill entrance. A Black woman stood inside a building with a window and scale in front to weigh the incoming loads. Normally, she would have waved him through, but today she stopped him. She had a police scanner inside the corrugated steel shack, and she undoubtedly heard what happened, but she most likely wanted the details too.

"What the hell happened over there?" She asked with her standard African American dialect that to him sounded southern, though he knew that she lived here all her life. Her face was a dark chocolate brown with the thick kinky "natural" hairstyle of the time. *Why she doesn't wear her hair normally like white people is beyond me,* he always said.

"Old Joe got shot by some asshole he pissed off trying to sell him house wiring stolen from a job site."

"Oh, sweet Jesus, that's terrible. Is it really bad?"

"He's dead and the guy who shot him got away, but not before Old Joe put some buck shot in him. The cops know who he is and it's just a matter of time before they nail him."

"Oh, that poor old man; I hope, when they catch him, they hang his hide."

"I hope so too. I had better get down there to see how Fat Fred is coming along. I'll talk at you later."

He put the van in gear and drove to the fill site. It always smelled of garbage, a smell unlike any other of decomposing food, animals and household refuse; a combination of many smells rolled into overwhelming stench. Fred always wore a paper mask, so he would not have to keep smelling it constantly. Unfortunately for his wife, who had to wash his clothes every day, she didn't have the luxury of a breathing respirator to rescue her from the stench that Mark felt certain overwhelmed the laundry room situated in one of the outbuildings behind their house.

Mark caught sight of Fred, a rotund forty-year-old man with a flat top hairstyle that made his paunch stand out more. Jay, a part time worker who came to the site after school wearing baggy jeans with collar length blonde hair, dug about in a freshly dumped pile of trash that rose up a vertical line up the hill from where the dumpster disposed its contents. The CAT operator waited patiently for them as they scoured the pile for recyclables.

Mark parked the van near where Fred had set up his most recent cache, next to his red and white two-toned Buick Skylark. Fred saw him, then gave the CAT operator the all-clear signal as the 973D Caterpillar Waste Loader moved the two or three cubic yards of waste down the pit. Later, Fred and Jay would revisit the pile to scavenge what they could not get earlier.

"What the hell happened over there, Mark?" Fred asked his face red with anger, as he seemed to get right into Mark's face, not so much to be a jerk, but to be heard above the roar of the CAT pushing the trash down the pit.

"Old Joe pissed off some asshole trying to sell him stolen house wiring. He left initially, then came back and killed Joe. Old Joe shot him with Bessie and they know who done it because Old Joe wrote down his license plate number; it is just a matter of time now," Mark explained in a very loud voice.

"And what about what the detective told me? That you tried to steal cash from Old Joe's cash drawer and blame it on the guy that shot him?"

"He told you?"

"Hell yeah, he told me. I can't trust you anymore, Mark. Go ahead take the rest of the day off. Take my car, and I'll load the van."

Mark felt uncertain what his future with Fred was. "I'm sorry I disappointed you, Fred. I actually did it for you."

"Yeah, that's what the detective told me. I don't need that kind of help. That kind of help lands people in prison. I don't want to spend the rest of my life in prison because of people like you trying to help. Go ahead and find Old Joe's killer and then come back and talk with me."

"Does the hare-lip know anything?"

"No, and if you take care of this, he'll never know. Stop calling him that, his name is Jay."

"Okay, Fred, I'll do that." Mark went to the '64 Buick Skylark and got behind the wheel, put it in drive and drove out from the landfill and down the gravel road to Fred's house. His thoughts felt jumbled and he could not organize them into a coherent and practical plan. *I need help, but whose?*

Metamorphoses

Mark walked two miles into town, called West Richland, formally named Enterprise, though Mark had no idea when, before one of his buddies honked at him and pulled over on Van Giessen Street and picked him up. Mark recognized the pearl-white custom '77 Monte Carlo with swivel seats as Dave Baker's ride.

"Hey there, Mark, what the hell are you doing? Get in and I'll get you where you think you need to go." Mark didn't hesitate and knew that if Dave could help find Kurt Jackson, especially if they ever did business together, would make it a whole lot easier on him. He shook Dave's hand as soon as he got inside the car.

Dave's most distinguishing feature was a shark tooth on a gold chain that hung down from his neck. He always tied back his long blonde hair in a ponytail. He wore prescription-tinted glasses and he had a smile on his clean-shaven face, even when he felt he had to beat the crap out of someone that owed him money.

His body looked lean and athletic because he did Karate and worked out religiously to stay in shape, and next to his driver's side console, sat a Colt.45. Because the local radio stations played nothing but crap, Dave had an eight-track system installed so he could listen to rock tunes such as Led Zeppelin, Eric Clapton and Aero Smith.

"I need your help Dave," Mark started to say.

"Sure, I think. What kind of help?"

"I need help finding somebody."

"Who?" Dave asked his friend with a side-long glance as he pulled out onto Van Giessen Street, the main drag of this town of eleven hundred people.

"Kurt Jackson."

"He's bad news, Mark. What do you need him for?"

"He killed Old Joe at Tommy Boy's Salvage this morning and I was there. I promised Old Joe I would take care of the bastard."

"Hell, I would find out where he lives and meet him there," Dave replied with his familiar smile that sometimes put Mark on edge because he was never certain what Dave was thinking.

"I'm sure the cops have that place pretty much pinned down."

"Well, I rarely have anything to do with him, Mark. I tend to do my dealings with people like you that wants a little recreational high occasionally."

"I guess what I'm asking you, is to help me find this asshole and help me take him out; I know it's a lot because it could get you in trouble too."

"That is asking a lot. I don't want to do prison time over an asshole like that. He has a lot of friends and associates that are already in the prison system. When they catch wind that he was taken out, and the person that did it is in the system too, my death sentence has already been handed to me," Dave replied as Mark caught a look of complete sincerity on his face for the first time.

"I see." Mark was quiet for a moment when he asked Dave, "Have you ever watched a person, who was very much alive a second ago, die in front of you?"

"I can't say that I have," Dave replied.

"It's eerie, man. It's almost like you're witnessing his soul leave his body. He asked me to do this one last thing for him and I promised I would do that. I just don't know the guy that I'm after. I don't know who he hangs out with or where he hides out at," Mark emphasized.

"If all you're looking for is a starting point to steer you in the right direction, then I'll help you there," Dave replied. "But the moment bullets start flying, you're on your own."

"Thanks a lot, Dave, you are really cool to help me out this way. Where are we going? You just passed my house."

"To our first location; he's a heroin dealer I know who may know where Kurt might be hiding out."

"Well, I appreciate that, but I wanted to shower and get out of these clothes first."

"Okay, okay, how about we stop at JC Penny and I'll buy you some clothes and anti-perspirant? I have to warn you though. The deeper we go here, the creepier and scarier these people we encounter are. Some of them, we may not be able to meet until after the witching hour because they do their best business then. You may not like what you see, and you may have a totally different attitude toward this town once we're done here," Dave told his best friend.

"I can understand that. Do I need to buy a gun?"

"As long as you keep quiet and do as I tell you, you should be all right. I have my 'Sweet Persuader' here beside me too," Dave stated with his familiar smile on his face.

Mark considered malls a blight on towns and cities because it took the people away from downtown, the heart of any community, as he preferred going to stores and shops in the older downtown area because it seemed more nostalgic, like going back in time. He so wished he could go back to relive those simpler days. He didn't care for this materialistic time and this post-Watergate crap with crooked politicians getting caught doing stupid things that he didn't understand.

I need to reinvent myself, he said to himself, as they left the highway and entered the exit to Columbia Center Boulevard.

They arrived, and the mall's parking lot appeared empty save for a dozen or, so cars scattered about here and there. None of the cars here looked any newer than Dave's, Mark guessed, as he assumed these cars belonged to the employees that worked there. Like Mark, they probably lived with their parents and made barely enough to get by, and paid cash from last year's tax return to buy their used piece of shit Chevy, Ford, Gremlin or Dodge.

They walked through the double doors and went up the escalator to where the men's clothing line hung from hangers or neatly stacked on shelves. Mark chose a sized 44 long double-breasted jacket and slacks made from Hager. He found blue pin striped shirt from Arrow and paisley tie, along with a brown leather belt to fit his 43-inch waist. He found some size 13AA penny loafers that fit snugly on his feet. He went to the dressing room, removed all the tags, and dressed himself to look like a character from a cheap detective dime novel.

Dave flashed the pretty cashier his wad of fifties and handed her two bills to cover the charge. He drove Mark to a drug store located on the west entrance of the mall, where they purchased deodorant, toothpaste and toothbrush.

While Dave drove to this first of presumably many contacts, Mark busied himself with getting the stench taken off his body and looking decent enough. "I feel like I'm missing something," Mark told Dave. "Can we go someplace that sells hats?"

"What kind of hat?" Dave asked with a dubious tone.

"A fedora would be perfect, I think."

"Are you trying to be like Mike Hammer or something?"

"No, not really; I just want to affect a certain image of myself that will send everyone I meet a message that I'm not to be messed with."

"Well, you may also have negative reaction where no one would want to talk to you," Dave replied, keeping his eyes on the increasingly heavy traffic congestion as the three o'clock rush began. "Or worse, get your ass kicked by someone that don't respect what you're doing."

"If that happens, and this is the reason why, then I'll modify my look a little," Mark reasoned as if he knew what he was talking about.

Dave didn't say anything more as he turned off the highway and onto Columbia Drive, passed used car lots that boasted this to be Auto Row, and then drove into the downtown parkade area of Kennewick. Dave found a hat store and parked his Monte Carlo in front.

Mark thought the place closed because he didn't see any cars parked nearby the shop. He tentatively pulled himself out from the car and walked to the door, but the sign welcomed them inside. He walked in with Dave in tow.

Mark saw many varieties and colors of hats, when he came upon a black, wide brimmed fedora like the one Humphrey Bogart might have worn in Casa Blanca or the Maltese Falcon. He put the hat on his head and liked how it looked in the full-length mirror. The hat fit his seven-and-a-half-inch head perfectly and enhanced his eyes even more. *I should do something about this hair and sideburns though,* he said to himself. "I'll take this one."

"You look like a mobster from one of those black and white movies from the '30s," Dave pointed out in criticism.

"That's the effect I'm after. The kind of people I need to talk to may not take me seriously if I wore regular street clothes. Looking like this, I have a chance to instill an edge over them and they'll feel like they have no choice but to respect me and tell me what I need to know."

"I hope you're right," Dave replied as doubt crossed his voice. "Personally, I think the opposite; but hey, what do I know."

Dave paid the elderly man behind the cash register, which also looked like something from the forties, as he methodically rung up the sale with arthritic fingers. "Well, you definitely look good with that fedora there," he stated in amazement as he picked up the fifty-dollar bill and said, "I'm sorry young man, but I can't break this here bill; I ain't got that much in my till."

Dave took the bill back, searched his wallet, and counted out the exact amount charged on the till and handed it to the elderly man with liver spotted hands. "Is there anything else, Mark?" Dave asked sounding more like an impatient husband following his wife through the boutiques and shops.

"I need a haircut," Mark replied looking at himself in the mirror and making a face of disgust at his own appearance.

"Bob's is just up the street," the old man volunteered. "He only charges three dollars too."

"Well thank you sir," Mark replied. "Let's go to see Bob the barber."

"Fine; you know I was just kidding. You seem to be wasting a lot of time doing this," Dave told his friend of twelve years.

"I know you were kidding, but I need to get my hair cut, or they won't take me seriously. Besides, you told me that most of the people we need to talk to aren't even awake yet," he replied as they left the small store and walked to Dave's car. Dave got in, started the car, backed out from the diagonal parking space, and drove west to Bob's Barbershop.

Two swivel barber chairs took up most of the space of this small shop, but only one was ever used because most men chose to wear long hair in the style of Andy Gibbs.

Mark's long hair made him appeared more like Dustin Hoffman's portrayal of Charging Bear in "Little Big Man." A smattering of Marine Corp paraphernalia dotted the walls of the small shop, including the Marine Corp motto, Semper Fidelis, hung on the wall over the barber chair closest to the wall where they saw a middle-aged man spring into action from the unused chair.

The barber had a flat top style that made him look like a Marine Gunnery sergeant. His face seemed chiseled from granite with hard lines and wrinkles that made a perfect fit for his salt, and pepper hair with block shaped head. "My God, two actual customers that are under thirty," Bob exclaimed in a deep booming baritone. "Who's my first victim?"

"Me, and I want your haircut," Mark responded, as he took a seat in the brown leather chair.

"What about you?" Bob asked Dave. "You feel brave enough to get that pretty ponytail cut off and get a real man haircut," Bob asked with a wry grin on his face.

"Hell, no I am not getting no haircut," Dave replied. "I have a reputation to keep."

"Suit yourself," Bob replied. "What's the occasion? You lost a bet or something?"

"Something like that," Mark answered, being purposefully evasive as he witnessed Bob throw a linen cloth over his front and wrap paper tissue around his neck. "You want to keep the mutton chops?" The former Marine asked.

"No, take them off too."

"That would be a dollar extra."

"That's fine," Mark replied patiently as he watched the older barber try to comb his bushy and thick brown hair back. He gave up on that notion, pulled out the electric razor and began buzzing the hair from Mark's head.

Mark saw bunches of hair fall from his head and land on his lap as the hair cut lasted maybe two minutes. Bob pulled out a straight razor that he honed on a strop. He lathered the side burns and then quickly removed the whiskers, leaving Mark's face smooth and youthful looking. He turned Mark around and showed him the result of Bob's labors.

Mark still never liked how he looked in mirrors; considering himself too ugly as he observed his hooked nose, broken in a bar fight last year celebrating his twenty-first birthday, and his one brown eye and one hazel eye made him appear freakish. Mark placed the fedora on his head and told Dave, "That's perfect. Pay him."

"I take it you don't have change for a fifty neither?"

Bob looked at Dave with a surprised look and said, "Hell no, I don't got no change for a fifty. This ain't no fancy hair salon at the mall, for crying out loud."

Dave handed him a ten and said, "Keep the change."

Looking for Kurt Jackson

The US Highway 12 offered a natural boundary between the affluent and white West Pasco and the poorer, minority dominated East Pasco as the Sunset Mobile Home Park, located just west, outside Pasco city limits, seemed pristine enough with newly built doublewides perched on lots where newly seeded Blue and Rye grass lawns began to germinate. But to Mark, the place just seemed like another trailer park occupied by trailer trash. Mark read the brochure last year when it was advertised as the latest advancement in family living at affordable prices.

Dave drove his Monte Carlo onto the opened gated area and took a right that led them down a narrow lane. Most driveways that bordered these lots with their aluminum-sided Marlette's and Fleetwood's were empty, more than likely because these people had real jobs and were making an honest living somewhere and hadn't made it home yet. Dave stopped alongside a blue and white two-tone Marlette with a large bay window, its drapes opened for a full view.

"This is where his heroin dealer lives?" Mark asked in shocked surprise.

"No, this is where someone that knows his heroin dealer lives. We'll meet his dealer soon enough," Dave explained to him as he still couldn't believe what Mark did, or why he even did it.

Mark didn't say anything, but felt his patience beginning to erode. *This better not be a complete waste of my time,* he said to himself. A varnish finished pine deck influenced the home's exterior décor, as both young men walked up the single step up to the deck, then another step that put them at the front door. Dave knocked, and they heard rustling inside, along with a steady beat of footfalls that became louder until they stopped, and the door opened.

The man, around five feet four and medium build, looked very unassuming as Mark sized him up. The only distinguishing feature that gave Mark a second glance was a jagged scar that ran along his jaw up his cheek, just stopping just short of his left eyelid. The mostly bald man looked up at Mark with suspicion. "Can I help you?"

"Nate, he's with me," Dave tried to reassure him.

"Well, introduce me to him, dumb shit."

Mark seemed impressed with this little man. He apparently had no fear, or he acted fearless quite well.

"Nate-Mark; Mark-Nate; are you satisfied, asshole?"

"Abundantly," as he offered his hand to Mark. Mark grabbed it and shook it firmly. Nate applied equally firm pressure. "I still want to know what you want."

"Well Nate…" Dave began.

"What the fuck? He can't speak for himself? Are you a deaf mute?" Nate demanded as his face turned crimson with anger.

"No, I'm not," Mark replied neutrally.

"Then tell me what the fuck you want," Nate commanded in frustration.

"I'm looking for someone."

"Will you stop with this fucking game? Who are you looking for and what does that have to do with me?"

"Kurt Jackson and we thought you may know him through his dealer," Mark replied quickly.

"Yeah, I know that son of a bitch. He's not someone you would want to fuck with," Nate told Mark. "He's crazy like most of us are normal. So, what do you want him for?"

"Well, I want to kill him," Mark replied with quiet determination.

"You'd have to stand in line. You see this?" He asked pointing at the scar on his face. Mark nodded.

"Well, he gave that to me when I wouldn't loan him money for an eight ball. I turned around and stuck him with my butterfly knife, but it didn't faze him. He just laughed and walked away. That was five years ago. I want him dead too. I don't know where the hell he is.

"Dave, you could try to contact Carlos, but I wouldn't recommend taking him with you," Nate emphasized jerking his head toward Mark.

Mark chose to ignore the implication that he was just insulted, while he stood there staring at the little man. "I think we're done here, Dave," Mark stated without malice.

"Well, I'll call him to let him know you're on the way, Nick stated to both. Nice meeting you, Mark." They shook each other's hands and Mark left with Dave as the door closed behind them. Dave drove away from the glamorous trailer park and headed east into Pasco.

Pasco, named for a mining town in Chile from the railroad baron that set up a switchyard back in the early twentieth century had the atmosphere of any mid-sized town of 14,000 residents. Mark could care less about that. He saw Pasco, the way most white people who didn't live there, as a slum where the blacks and the illegal aliens lived. He felt his heart pounding harder as he automatically locked his car door to prevent someone from trying to get in. He glanced down between the seats to ensure Dave's .45 Colt was still within reach. He always felt a twinge of anxiety when coming into this part of Tri-Cities.

He heard the stories from his parents after they moved him and his two older sisters here from Wenatchee in 1968. Those stories included race riots, robberies and shootings among neighborhood gangs that roamed Pasco seemingly at will. He heard how white women were not safe and only prostitutes would be brave enough to come into this town. Mark believed these stories to be true and relayed them to other white people of like mindset, who would nod at Mark knowingly in agreement.

Dave drove the car down Court Street toward the switch yard, turning right onto North 1st, and left onto Sylvester just a few blocks from the National Guard Armory in front of a house with cars parked in the weed infested dirt yard. Weeds grew around the cars as if they were part of the ambience.

The cars themselves looked like they hadn't run in years, and one that looked like a Studebaker was on blocks, its engine lying on the ground next to it as oil stained the ground like a black blotch. Dave stopped and turned off the ignition, as he started to get out.

"You're not taking your gun?" Mark asked in horror.

"No, I'm not. Why should I?" Dave asked incredulously at Mark.

"Because this is Pasco," Mark replied, waving his hand universally in the air.

"And your point?" Dave asked frustrated by Mark's attitude.

"Are you kidding me? This place is full of crime and people who commit crimes. You can't trust anyone here," Mark replied to Dave as if he was a half-wit.

"I've done business here and I've never had problems. I have this gun for show more than anything else. I don't like packing inside someone's pad, it's too tempting for people to get really nervous," Dave explained.

"I'm sorry, but I don't trust those people," Mark stated.

Dave grinned in frustration at Mark and walked toward the door, leaving Mark behind in the car with his .45 Colt automatic. Dave knocked on the door and a young brown-skinned girl opened the door briefly, and then closed it. *I hate that brown-skinned girl,* Mark said bitterly to himself.

Dave waited a moment when a thin, almost anemic-looking Hispanic man with long black hair and sunglasses to shield his eyes from the late afternoon sun, stepped outside and they embraced each other briefly. Mark listened in on the conversation from the partially opened passenger side window.

"Amigo querido, what do I owe this visit?" Carlos asked his long-time friend.

"Carlos, I have a favor to ask."

"You know I owe you my life and you only need to ask," Carlos stated in Spanish accented English quite familiar to Mark, piquing Mark's curiosity.

"I appreciate that you remembered. I need to find someone you may know. He's malasnoticias. I believe you do business with him."

"Are you referring to a man that may be wanted for killing Old Joe?" Carlos asked, and Mark determined he knew and more than likely had him inside the house. *That bastard*, Mark thought.

"My friend, sitting in the car is searching for him."

"Is he a vigilante?"

"Yes, he and Old Joe were amigos," Dave replied.

"I don't want trouble with my family. So please, I will send Kurt somewhere, so they can meet away from mi casa."

"Can you drop him off to someplace away from here?" Dave asked Carlos Lopez.

"Si, go to the Top Hat at ten tonight. We will meet there." They embraced briefly and shook hands and Carlos waited at the door while Dave walked to the car. He continued to watch as they drove down the two-lane street.

"So, you speak their lingo?" Mark asked suspiciously.

"Yeah, Mark and I also sleep with their women," Dave replied in exasperation.

"That's what is wrong with this country. This is an American country where American should be the only language of the land, not some foreign language that I can't understand," Mark responded in frustration. Dave stared at him briefly and shook his head as he continued, "We're going to meet them tonight at the Top Hat at ten."

"What time is it now?"

"It's six right now," Dave replied as he glanced quickly at his watch.

"Then that son of a bitch is hiding out in that wet back's house," Mark railed passionately.

"So, what if he is? I promised Carlos we wouldn't get his family involved in this. We'll meet at the place and time I promised him."

He stewed in silent rage. "I need to eat something. I'm really getting hungry. Can we stop at a Denny's or something?"

"Sure, I can do that. I think there's one up on 20th just up from Court Street."

"Not in Pasco," he protested. "Let's go to the Denny's by the mall. I don't know what those people put in the food here."

Dave looked at his friend with a feeling of increasing frustration and impatience. "What the hell is your problem, man?"

"Nothing is wrong with me." Mark thought a moment before replying. "I am who I am, Dave. I don't like this town; it's full of the kind of people I don't like or trust. I came from a town where there were no colored people; then I wind up here, where there are all kinds of those people, and most are criminals."

"All I can tell you, Mark, is get used to it if you plan to make it in this world. I guess if you want to be a hermit, and live in complete isolation somewhere, you could survive and live alone from what you fear."

"Oh, I don't fear anything. You're right though, I plan to find someplace away from here where I don't have to deal with them. I miss the good old days where segregation was the law of the land and a good old lynching was as commonplace as an afternoon baseball game."

"Well, okay then just be aware that I plan to talk to people, who are minorities, who more than likely know Kurt Jackson and what his habits are. They would just assume kick the crap out of you than put up with your racist views. So, if you are serious about finding this Jackson guy, you had better keep your views to yourself," Dave said as his familiar smile disappeared, replaced by a mask of anger.

"What was it that he said about you owing him his life?" Mark asked intentionally throwing the subject away from him and back at Dave.

"Four and a half years ago, I saved his life when another dealer named Salazar, tried to muscle in on the local pot market. He did it by trying to put a hit on Carlos. Me and Kurt took him out. Fat Fred helped us by opening the landfill for us, so we could dispose the guy's body. No one needs to know about this, Mark. Is that clear?"

Mark nodded as they took the exit going from downtown Pasco to the US 12 freeway. He glanced briefly at his friend and realized for the first time, that he really didn't know him.

Che and Carlos Lopez' Conversation

After Carlos saw Dave's car disappear down Sylvester Street, he went to his phone sitting on the coffee table, cluttered with crayons, grocery lists, discarded bills and a coloring book, and dialed the phone number to his father, Che Lopez, head of the Lopez Cartel of Todos Santos, Mexico. He immediately didn't like the idea that someone was snooping about wanting to know what happened at the junkyard where that old man named Joe was shot. He especially didn't like his friend Dave helping this person go after Kurt Jackson.

He heard his father's unmistakable voice come across through the scratchy background noise that most likely was some American government's attempt at a wiretap, but that was to be expected, considering the business activities they chose to engage in. In the other room, down the hall, Carlos could hear Kurt Jackson moaning loudly as Carlos' wife tried nursing his gunshot wound. He could only imagine how she was pouring rubbing alcohol upon the bleeding wound and bandaging it to help ease the bleeding.

"What do I owe this pleasure, my son?" His father asked after Carlos identified himself. It had been five years since

Carlos set up his distribution business in Pasco, and five years since he last saw his adopted father.

"I have a problem, Father; I need some father to son advice," he replied to Che Lopez. The silence on the other end seemed deafening, and Carlos knew his father was waiting for the story to come out from his lips.

"I see," he replied slowly in a deliberate manner. "Is it business related to our distribution network?"

Carlos swallowed hard, as he tentatively replied, "Not in so many words, no it isn't."

"Tell me more, please," Che told his son, hinting that his patience had begun to wane.

"There was an incident between an old man at a local junk yard and one of my mules. He attempted to sell stolen household wiring for the copper value, when the old man called the police. He left initially, coming here and I went back with him. That stupid old man refused to listen to reason and he got shot."

"Were there witnesses?"

"No, Papa, the old man was the only one I saw in the shop," Carlos replied as he felt his underarms dripping from sweat.

"Is there another problem then?"

"Yes, apparently there's a friend of this old man who wants retribution for what happened to him."

"What is his name?"

"I don't know, but I told my friend, Dave Baker; he's the one who saved me from Cesar Salazar four and a half years ago; anyway, I told him to bring this person to a local dive called the Top Hat," Carlos explained quickly to his father. "He wants Kurt Jackson."

"I take it that's your mule, si?"

"Si," Carlos replied.

"It's quite simple, my son. You must eliminate the problem, before it becomes a bigger problem. Goodbye Carlos."

Informing Detective Dickerson

They crossed over the Columbia River Bridge into Kennewick as he cruised down US Route 12 to the mall entrance where the Denny's Restaurant stood just off the right of the entrance of Columbia Center Boulevard; once they entered the restaurant, Mark excused himself. "I need to piss and wash up; I'll be right with you." When he had finished, he went to a bank of pay phones, threw in fifteen cents, and called the number off the detective's business card.

"This is Detective Dickerson."

"Mark Marteau, he's going to meet us at The Top Hat at ten tonight," he replied in a low audible tone that was barely over a whisper.

"What? I can hardly hear you. Who is this?"

"I'm at a Denny's in Kennewick by the mall, he continued in the low voice."

"Who are you?"

Goddammit, Mark said to himself in frustration. "It's Mark Marteau," he replied an octave higher, but still low enough to where no one could over hear the conversation.

"Okay, I got that now. You sound like Mark, is that correct?"

"Yeah, it's Mark. He's gonna meet us at the Top Hat around ten tonight with some Spic named Carlos."

"Carlos, you say; is his last name Lopez?" Detective Dickerson asked.

"I don't know what his last name was," Mark replied.

"I want you there to make it look good. Then, I want you make up some excuse and walk away; we'll take over from there."

"When do I get my reward," Mark asked.

"When we arrest him," Detective Dickerson replied.

"I'll see you then." He hung up the phone and saw Dave standing there. "Fuck, man you scared the shit out of me."

"Who was that?" Dave asked suspiciously.

"It's a girl I'm trying to get a date with," Mark lied with a straight face.

"Really?" Dave asked. "I hope you get your girl then. I must call Nicole. We're in the booth over in the non-smoking area."

"Non-smoking? I haven't had a smoke all day and I'm jonesing for a ciggy," Mark complained.

"Well, I don't smoke, and you can go over there at the coffee counter to have your smoke. I'm not moving to the smoking section for your nasty habit," Dave said with conviction.

He didn't bother to argue his logic, went over to the coffee counter, and lit up a cigarette while he waited for Dave to finish his call. *Finally, I'll be done with this and can get back to working for Fred again. What the hell am I thinking? I don't want to keep doing the same old thing again. I hate doing this job, but I need to be doing something more meaningful than collecting junk from a landfill. I kind of liked doing this, though. Maybe I'll ask Dickerson how I should go about getting a job doing this kind of work,* he said to himself.

Dave came back, walked past him, and headed toward the designated non-smoking section.

Mark quickly snuffed out the remaining cigarette in the glass ashtray that sat between upside down cups and saucers, as the middle-aged waitress, who stood behind the counter, smiled politely at Mark expecting a tip for occupying her counter. Mark ignored her and went to the booth where Dave sat.

Mark sat across from him, picked up a menu, and began reading it. Dave scanned the menu and laid it back down on the table as he fiddled nervously with a teaspoon.

"Is there something wrong, Dave?"

"No man, I'm just a little nervous about this meeting."

"He's your friend," Mark responded angrily. "Why should you be nervous?"

"Are you ready to order?" A cute twenty-year-old waitress, who was destined to be just like the waitress behind the counter, smiled sweetly over her order-pad with pencil at the ready. She wore her blonde hair pinned back. Her smock appeared neatly pressed and her nametag read *Cindi*.

"I'll have a grilled cheese sandwich and a coffee," Dave replied.

"I want the steak and eggs with hash browns and whole-wheat toast."

"How do you want your eggs?"

"Over-easy," he replied.

"How do you want your steak?"

"Rare."

"Would you like anything to drink?"

"I'll have a whiskey and beer back," Mark replied smugly.

"Can I see your ID?" Cindi asked Mark with a sweetie-pie voice.

"Of course," Mark replied as he pulled out his wallet from his back pocket and handed her the plastic drivers' license. She smiled amiably and handed it back to him.

"I'll bring your drinks out to you." She left them and handed the ticket to the assistant manager, who went inside the lounge to prepare Mark's drink.

Their meals arrived ten minutes later, along with Mark's drink. Mark did his shot and began preparing his steak and eggs by drowning everything in steak sauce, including the hash browns. He then cut the meat into small bits, and then began chewing on his meal quietly.

Dave, on the other hand, had finished eating the grilled cheese sandwich before Mark was halfway through cutting his meat, and then he deliberately chewed each bite of steak carefully. It took him almost half an hour before he pushed the empty plate away and finished drinking down the beer.

Dave left a two-dollar tip on the table and they went to pay the waitress with the big bee hive hairdo standing behind the counter. Dave paid her, and they left the restaurant.

The Meeting

At ten o'clock, they arrived at the Top Hat, an old greasy spoon restaurant on Lewis Street in the heart of down town Pasco. It sat on a corner street and used to be a going concern back in its day, but now just about every low life in town came here to meet to do the deals that the cops appeared helpless to prevent. Mark and Dave walked in through the entrance and continued to the back to the lounge. Between the restaurant and the lounge, were the men's' and women's restrooms, that reeked of overuse and disinfectant. The lounge, purposefully kept dimly lit, took both men awhile to adjust their eyes.

A pair of pool tables with brightly lit overhead lights with green shade appeared in a far corner from the bar as two black women shot a game of eight ball.

They sat down at a table and waited for Carlos and Kurt Jackson to arrive. Dave suddenly stood up and announced, "I need to take a piss. I'll be right back."

"You're leaving me alone here, with these people?" Mark asked in horror as Dave could see the fear in his eyes. "You can't do that!"

"I'm sorry man," Dave said sincerely and left.

Mark was going to get up and follow him, when he heard a familiar voice, "Are you looking for me?"

It startled him as he quickly turned around and saw Kurt Jackson, half stooped over and clearly in pain standing in front of him.

"It's not just me that's looking for you. You seem to have a knack for pissing off a lot of people that would love nothing better than to see you six feet under," Mark stated to Kurt with menace in his voice. "I'm one of them!"

"You weren't there; you didn't see who did it. I just came in to try to reason with him. You don't want to know who did it. You wouldn't believe me if I told you."

Mark looked at him in disbelief and asked, "Who did it then?"

"It was Da…"

A shot rang out behind Mark that was clearly a large caliber handgun and caused him to drop down to the floor, burying his head instinctively. Mark rose up when he realized he was still very much alive, but he heard Kurt gasping for air, trying to find his last ounce of breath to finish telling Mark who shot Old Joe.

"Come on man, let's get out of here," Dave said to Mark, dragging him to his feet. Mark did not have time enough to figure out what Kurt was trying to tell him, as Dave kept pushing him out the bar through a side door.

Police already converged on the bar. Mark felt suddenly surrounded and overwhelmed. Seemingly out of nowhere, officers seized both men as they tried to get into Dave's car; blocked in by two police cruisers, Dave and Mark were placed in handcuffs.

Detective Dickerson showed up out from the dark. "I thought I told you to walk away, that we would take care of everything."

Dave looked at Mark thunder struck. "You're a fuckin' narc? I'll kill you, you bastard! I trusted you and you betrayed me."

Mark suddenly figured out what Kurt was trying to tell him. *He's right*, Mark thought, *I don't believe it.*

However, then he vaguely remembered the three shots that rang out. The first shot was high pitch pop sound, the second, because it came almost at the same time sounded like a shotgun blast, and the third sounded exactly like the shot that seemingly burst his eardrum when it struck Kurt. *On the other hand, was it the other way around?*

"I want to make a statement in the police station," Mark announced to the detective.

"Are you ready to confess then?"

"To what?" Mark demanded in defiance. "I didn't do anything!"

"We'll see. Take them both into custody," Tracey Dickerson said. "I will get to the bottom of this and one of you will be going to prison."

The Interrogation

Mark sat by himself in a room where a mirror pretty much encompassed the entire western wall. Mark knew cops were there watching him, waiting for him to sweat, and become restless and show his guilt without the police trying to get a confession out of him. Across from him, another chair and a bare table stood between the chair and him. A legal pad with pencil sat on the table in front of the vacant chair. Mark wasn't going to give them the pleasure of seeing him confess guilt without confessing.

He sat motionless, watching the notepad in front of him, concentrating on the yellow sheet with the straight black lines; eight and a half inches wide, 14 inches long.

What shade of yellow do they call this? Is it beige, or cream, lemon chiffon, light yellow, or just plain yellow? I'd say it's light yellow. But then again, the lighting in this room may have something to do with it. What about the pencil? It's a shade of yellow too. But I would guess it's a goldenrod kind of yellow. It's a long pencil perfectly sharpened with an automatic pencil sharpener. Who made this pencil? Mark couldn't tell what the brand on the pencil read.

Detective Dickerson walked into the interrogation room and eyed Mark but gave away nothing to him on what he thought about the young man in front of him. He sat down and began writing in the notepad. "By law I'm required to read you your Miranda rights. Do I need to call in an interpreter?"

"No, that won't be necessary."

"You have the right to be silent. Anything that you say, should you give up that right, will be used against you in the court of law. You have the right to an attorney. If you cannot afford an attorney, one will be granted to you by the court. Do you understand your Miranda rights?"

"Yes, I do."

"You said before I arrested you and brought you here, that you had a statement to make?"

"Yes, I do."

"Is this statement a confession?"

"No."

"Do you want me to call a lawyer for you to seek legal counsel before you make this statement?"

"No."

"Go ahead then. I'm all ears."

"When I told you, I heard two initial shots, then a bigger shotgun shot, at first, I didn't think much of it; that both shots sounded like they came from the same gun. But tonight, I heard the same shot I heard this morning coming from a bigger gun. I know I saw two wounds on Old Joe, but I didn't, nor couldn't distinguish round size. I'm sure your experts probably could, though."

Mark watched Detective Dickerson write this all down. He finished and looked up at Mark expecting him to start talking again. He knew he was leaning toward telling him what he needed to hear. "What else?"

"That's it. Except, I wouldn't release Dave right away, if I was you."

"Why is that?"

"Because I think he's Old Joe's killer."

"And your proof is?"

"I told you, the sounds I heard. Each gunshot was different, sounding like they came from different guns. The gun that Kurt had sounded like a popping noise; the shotgun I'm sure I heard second, and I figure that was Old Joe shooting Kurt; and the last shot I heard this morning, sounded like the shot I heard tonight coming from behind me that struck down Kurt at the Top Hat."

"And you're saying Dave did this?"

"Yes, and that Kurt told me he didn't do it and was about to tell me that Dave shot Old Joe before Kurt got shot."

"You must think I'm the biggest fool in the world. Come on, Mark, confess. You killed Joseph Murdock, didn't you?"

"How could I? I was talking to the dispatcher on the phone in his office when those shots rang out," Mark expressed to Detective Dickerson in a rising hysteria.

"Where's the gun, Mark? Is it still out in the junkyard somewhere?"

"I didn't have a gun, goddammit!"

"At first you were convinced it was Kurt Jackson; now you're saying it's your friend, Dave…His gun has never been fired—clean as a whistle. I'll let the judge go easy on you, I promise."

Mark's frustration had reached a fever pitch. "I didn't shoot Old Joe!"

"That's all well and good, but you just said yourself that the shot you heard tonight was behind you. All the witnesses I interviewed only saw you confronting Kurt and then a shot rang out."

Mark was starting to lose his cool disposition as he was being thrown into the fire of circumstantial evidence. "I didn't have a gun, though."

"Neither did Dave. So far, no weapon has been recovered. Until a weapon is found, I can't hold any one of you. All I have from Dave is the fact you wanted to find Kurt and you wanted to take him out, to avenge Old Joe's murder."

"Have the police checked the restrooms?"

"I have no idea. But I'll investigate it and get back with you. I will do you a favor and place him in a 72-hour hold."

"Thanks, I appreciate that."

"By the way, you said that Carlos was to be at the Top Hat too?"

"Yeah, that's right."

"Well, no witnesses I spoke with saw him there and his wife hasn't seen him all night either."

"That's interesting."

"Isn't it possible that Dave isn't the person either?"

"But Kurt started to say Dave, not Carlos."

"He may have been trying to protect Carlos."

Mark could see that, as he slowly calmed down from the earlier confrontation. *Was he testing me?* "I take it then that Carlos is your suspect?"

"At this point, there are no suspects; just persons of interest. Right now, I need to question Carlos…"

A knock at the door caused Detective Dickerson to get up from his chair and answer the door. A brief exchanged between the detective and the officer was hushed and brief. He closed the door and announced, "I have good news for you, Mr. Marteau. The gun that apparently shot Mr. Jackson was found, as you said, in the women's restroom under a stall, and a witness came forward to say a Hispanic male matching the description of Carlos Lopez was seen running from the scene."

A sense of relief overtook Mark because not only had they found the murder weapon, but also that he and Dave were cleared in this. However, he purposefully kept his emotions in check as he asked the detective, "What's next?"

"You're free to go, along with your friend. There's no reason for us to hold any of you now that we have Mr. Lopez in our sights."

Both men found themselves outside the police station on Clark Street in downtown Pasco. Mark knew he needed to talk with Dave because he needed him to drive him home. He checked his pride and called out to him as Dave started walking down the street to recover his car still parked at the Top Hat. "Dave, please wait up."

He didn't stop walking, but replied, "I have nothing to say to you."

"Look, I'm sorry I didn't tell you everything, but I also knew I couldn't have done this without your help," Mark watched him stop and turned around.

"That's what upsets me more than anything else," Dave replied in frustration. "You took advantage of me and my contacts. You violated a sacred trust."

"Well, Carlos pretty much violated that trust too."

"What do you mean?"

"He killed Jackson to keep him silent."

"No, he missed his target because I hit his arm just before he fired the gun."

Mark didn't know what to say to that. "I owe you my life then. Thanks friend."

"It's called friendship, Mark. I would think; even hope that you would do the same had the tables been turned."

Mark didn't answer right away. *Would I, could I do that?* "Well, duh; of course, I would. We've been through a lot in our twelve years of friendship," Mark said to Dave. Mark had finally caught up to Dave as he reached his car. "I still need to find Old Joe's killer."

"I thought Kurt Jackson was the killer."

"No, I'm convinced the killer was the same man that tried to kill me tonight."

"Are you sure? He's not one to mess with. I really think he's under the thumb of a Mexican drug lord. If you mess with him, you mess with an entire drug gang; that's probably why the cops never messed with him because of who he is and where he's ranked in that hierarchy."

"That don't change how I feel. The cops might be afraid of him, but I'm not. To me, he just another greaser that I would love nothing better than to take out," Mark stated with real determination.

Dave shook his head in a way that could be interpreted as disbelief. "He's also a friend of mine. You really have thrown me in a bind, not just because of our friendship, but also because of how this will look to my buyers. If I help you, I might as well close up shop and move away."

"Nobody knows anything yet. Just drop me off where you think he is and loan me your .45."

"No, I don't loan my persuader to anyone. I'm in it with you to the end. I'll enlist in the army or something. I need to get out of this line of work anyway. God knows whom this country will elect for our next president. He may be one of those super conservative types that wants to create a war on drugs."

The Confrontation

They climbed into the Monte Carlo and headed east on Lewis Street into the heart of East Pasco. Dave told Mark on the way, "I know a pair of hookers that Carlos hangs out with. They're really good looking and most likely from Mexico too."

"I take it you spent some time with them?"

"Yeah, I have," Dave replied. "Hey, I saved his life once and it was his way of paying me back. Please, don't tell Nicole."

Mark again looked at his best friend, like he was looking at a stranger, but nodded and said, "Sure, I promise."

He drove into a trailer court, down a dirt drive. Even at three in the morning, it seemed like every trailer had activity going on. The lights of each trailer illuminated brightly as a variety of characters came and went from each trailer. The trailers themselves looked like they came from another era; dilapidated, single wide with the tires still connected. Smoke billowed from opened windows and doors. Dave stopped at the end of the drive and shut off the engine. "This is it."

The trailer appeared unlike the others, made from stainless steel that looked streamlined and illuminated brightly off the early morning moonlight. "I like that trailer. Do you know what it's called?" Mark asked as he checked his fedora in the side view mirror.

"I believe it's an old Airstream trailer. It's big inside too and it's like 30 feet long," Dave said. He checked his full clip and then slid back the pistol's receiver of his .45 and pressed the slide button that pushed the action forward, placing a bullet in the chamber, and put the gun back inside his shoulder holster located inside his jacket of his right shoulder.

They stealthily moved from the car and slowly made their way to the door, using the shadows of the trees to conceal their movements. A single light shone from the back-bedroom window and mariachi music played off a stereo in the front of the trailer. Dave led the way as he knocked on the door.

"What the hell are you doing? Just bust down the door with guns a blazing," Mark whispered angrily.

"You really are a dipshit. The door is always locked and, the door pulls open on travel trailers."

"Oh, sorry I didn't know."

"Quién cuesta?" Carlos asked from the other side of the door.

"It's Dave, Carlos. Can you let me in?"

They heard the door unlock and opened out. "Come in Amigo. Welcome!"

Dave led the way and Mark slowly followed, not knowing what to expect. The front room appeared clean and tidy, as Mark glanced about and saw the kitchen was equally clean and tidy. He did not see anyone else in the trailer, which made the hairs in his neck stand straight up.

"I don't believe I've ever had the pleasure of meeting you, gringo."

"I'm Mark Marteau," though he wanted to add more, but a silent request from Dave; a slight head shake, told him to stay quiet. He appraised the man that tried to shoot him earlier. He measured him and looked for any vulnerability or weakness the man in front of him might possess. *He's short and thin, his bare chest showed little muscle tone. He looks weak and anemic.*

Mark knew this man hadn't survived this long without knowing how to take care of himself in this business. *He may look like a little man, but he must have an edge somewhere, speed or quickness? An ability to evade punches? Is there a knife in his back pocket? A gun stashed somewhere nearby? On the other hand, does he disarm with his charm and wit, only to cut your throat when your back is to him?* Both men gave each other steady gazes, as if measuring up prior to a prize fight.

"What do I owe this unannounced visit?" Carlos asked Mark, all but ignoring Dave as he smiled ruthlessly at him, showing his gold crowns.

"My friend, Mark would very much like you to turn yourself in for killing your friend Kurt," Dave replied.

"You are funny, amigo. Why should I turn myself in to the police?"

"Well..."

"No, Dave let him tell me why I should do such a thing," Carlos demanded as he attempted to stare down Mark.

He shows no fear, that might be the key, Mark thought. *He doesn't fear me, and as such he doesn't have respect for me, he might show a weakness that I can exploit, as when I used to wrestle in high school.* "I don't want any trouble with you. I realize you and Dave are friends, and that he saved your life four years ago. For his sake, I would hope you would do the right thing and turn yourself into the police and make a confession."

He started to giggle, and then laughed seemingly uncontrollably. "Stop, you're killing me amigo. I do not intend to turn myself in. I have too much at stake here. I'll tell you what I will do though." Mark saw the smile fade from his face and an ugly mask of anger and hatred replaced it.

"What is that?" Mark asked, bracing himself for whatever this man had in mind to do. The front door behind him was still opened. Should he attack, he could feign away from his attack and watch him fly out the door. He waited and watched the man make his first move.

"I will kill you for being stupid enough to come out here to find me, and then I will kill Dave for bringing you out here to confront me and showing no respect for who I am."

"I have a question to ask before you follow through with your threat, Carlos. Did you shoot and kill Old Joe too?" *Here it goes*, Mark said to himself.

"Yes, I knew Kurt was acting on his anger and wouldn't be able to place the fatal shot needed to send the message," Carlos Lopez replied, as his movement was quick and effortless. He launched a filleting knife at Dave.

Mark saw it and lunged at the knife to deflect its intended target. *I hope it hits hilt first*, he thought just as the blade stuck firm in his deltoid muscle. The one nestled between his clavicle and pectoral muscles. It seemed to paralyze his entire left arm, as the pain felt almost unbearable. "Ouch," Mark screamed out. "Shit, that hurts."

"You son of a bitch," he heard Dave say. Mark looked up to see Dave with that familiar smile on his face. This smile, though was born of anger and disappointment at his friend who missed his intended target because of what Mark had just done. He pulled out his Colt 1911.45 caliber semi-automatic from his shoulder holster, with his left hand, released the safety and fired two quick rounds at Carlos. They stood no more than two feet from each other.

Both bullets found their mark in Carlos' chest and the impact knocked him to the floor as Mark witnessed the third person in twenty-four hours die in front of him.

Mark heard a commotion of foreign tongues chattering in the other room and one naked girl came running out, her face, a mask of many emotions, holding a sawed-off shotgun that she fired at Dave. The pellets hit Dave hard on his torso and face from ten feet away.

The impact threw him out the opened door. She ran up to Mark, seemingly ready to shoot him too, but she hesitated as she saw the knife lodged firmly in his shoulder. Apparently, she assumed the knife had killed him. He was not dead.

He pulled the knife painfully, with full-throated scream from his bleeding shoulder, and sliced it across her abdomen. She fell forward to the floor clutching her stomach, screaming out her error as the shotgun fell to the floor next to Carlos. The trailer suddenly erupted with people screaming out orders as another blast from a gun sounded off in the back room. He then heard a scream come from another woman.

Independence Day

Mark lost consciousness and did not awaken again until later that morning. His mother and father stood over his hospital bed, visible concern for their son's welfare etched upon their middle-aged faces. He did not feel anything from his left shoulder. He tried to turn his neck to see the heavily bandaged wound, but a sudden searing pain stopped him in his tracks. He moaned out and then smiled, grateful to be alive. Then concern crossed his face as he asked, "Dave, how's Dave doing?"

"He's still in surgery. But he was conscious and demanding that they get to you first," his forty-year-old mother replied. "You both need to get your heads examined. The idea of getting involved in drug activity is asinine. I hope you two learned your lesson and quit that dope crap."

"Yeah, I have," he promised his rather plump, red headed mother.

Detective Dickerson came into the room, "Good morning, folks. I'm Detective Dickerson, and if you don't mind, I need to speak with the suspect about his involvement with what happened this morning."

He waited for them to hug their son and leave the room. "Well, Mark you have a lot of explaining to do. It's lucky for you I put a tail on you two. It very well would have ended a whole lot differently."

"Yeah, but it confirmed a lot about friendship. Does this mean I don't get my reward?"

"I don't believe I said that Mr. Marteau." He reached inside his gray suit's left breast pocket and handed him a folded check in his right hand. "It's for two hundred thousand dollars. The FBI and DEA had a warrant out for Mr. Lopez too. He was the number three man under a Mexican drug cartel operating in this country. This is like your luckiest day, Mark."

"No, this is my Independence Day."

Day of Mourning

Che Lopez received the news via a courier delivering a telegram from his daughter-in-law. The telegram dropped to the floor as Che cried out in sorrow, "Carlos!"

The telegram landed face up as it showed, "Carlos este muerte."

Ultimatum
15 October 2014

"Charlotte, Hector and I are going to Mexico to get Dylan before he does something stupid, like get himself killed," Mark told his fiancée as he changed from his bib overalls to his double-breasted suit and set his fedora on his head.

"You two are too old to be playing hero," Charlotte stated honestly, as she watched him pack an over-night bag and placed his .357 from his tackle box to the opened overnight nylon bag. "What if you two get yourselves killed? You know I couldn't live without you all the way out here." Her face, a middle-aged mixture of lines and fifty years of worry and confusion drawn out, became angry and determined.

"I'll be fine, and so will Hector. If what he is telling me is true, then we should be able to avert anything from happening. If anything does happen, everything will be in the safe and you'll be well taken care of." They walked outside the one room cabin. He kissed her tenderly and then he got into the driver's seat.

"That's fine Mark, but if you aren't back in forty-eight hours, I'll drive back to Kennewick, and I don't want to see you again," Charlotte stated giving no quarter to Mark.

Mark looked at her curiously, as he started up the Hemi V-8. "I'll be back. Hector, get in; I'm driving this time."

End

Hotel California
15 October 2014

Mark drove down the county road heading southwest toward the two-lane highway that would take them to Missoula Airport, and eventually, to Todos Santos, Mexico. He remembered Charlotte's last words to him before they kissed each other goodbye. It seared into his mind like a white-hot brand, *"You have forty-eight hours to complete your business, or I'll go back to Kennewick, and I don't want to see you again."*

He glanced momentarily at his partner and noticed how much he had aged since the first time they met; how much bigger his gut had become; how much greyer his hair had turned and how many more wrinkles Hector had since they first met each other in 1987. "We're too damn old to be doing this shit, Hector."

Hector nodded as he took in the beauty of Western Montana, seemingly for the first time. Mark imagined he was too busy driving up here from Missoula to notice the high mountain peaks whose glacial peaks gave the national park its name. The tops reflected the rising sun as the early morning shadows slowly disappeared to harken a new day. Hector saw Elk grazing in the tall grass in an open meadow.

"Remember our first road trip down there, Mark?"

"Yeah, I remembered," Mark, replied remembering the day that he got the call that still haunted him.

1 July 1987

Dylan Baker played with his Hot Wheels car, a replica of a 1981 Chevrolet Camaro just like his daddy, Dave Baker who would arrive home soon, as his four-year-old ears listened intently outside for the distinctive sound of his car rolling into the driveway.

He pretended Daddy was inside the Hot Wheels car as he raced home to his imaginary house, a shoebox with colored windows and door that opened out while Mommy made flowers from yellow and red construction paper and helped Dylan paste it to the imaginary home.

The sun beat hot on this July day, 1987 and he played inside the doublewide Daddy said he bought several years ago with the reward money he split with Uncle Mark after they found Old Joe's killer. Although young Dylan didn't totally understand the concept of who Old Joe was or what a killer was, but to Dylan, Daddy and Uncle Mark were heroes.

His soft blonde hair, pulled back in a long ponytail like Daddy's, appeared almost white, with the texture of spun silk. His blue eyes were big and wide and resembled Mommy's whom Dylan learned was Nicole. His former chubbiness of toddler stage began to pass as he became taller and slimmer.

He wore big boy underwear that made him proud that he was no longer a baby and went potty without Mommy or Daddy watching over him. Today he dressed himself in his favorite Osh-Kosh-be Gosh blue pull-up shorts and red and white striped t-shirt. His little knees had battle scars from falling off a slide at a nearby park recently of scabbed over lacerations.

He heard the rumbling sound emitted into the living room, even though the stereo played a Madonna song that Mommy enjoyed, but Daddy hated. He immediately stopped playing with his Hot Wheels Camaro and ran to the door just ahead of Mommy, who he thought was the prettiest Mommy in the whole world, though his friend Trevor's mommy was a close second. He opened the door and just noticed a black car roll up to the front of their house but ignored it when he saw Daddy parked the Camaro and walked leisurely along a brick walkway toward the two steps that led to the door.

"Daddy!" Dylan screamed enthusiastically as he felt Mommy pulling him back.

"Dylan, how many times have I told you not to run outside like that," he heard her scold him.

He grabbed Daddy's pants leg to hug him when he heard a voice ask, "Are you Dave Baker?"

The voice sounded with an accent he never heard before, and he turned around, curious as to whom this person was that asked Daddy's name. He didn't have much more than an opportunity at a glance.

Daddy yelled, "Get in the house, now!" Daddy pushed him and Mommy back inside and slammed the door on them. He and Mommy ran to the big window that saw their favorite tree and the green lawn that Daddy always watered early in the morning before going to work at Seven Eleven and mowed on his day off.

Dylan saw two men, brown-skinned wearing black shiny coats that ended just past their knees. They had black pants and black shoes and wore sunglasses. One was fat and had gold teeth that flashed when he grinned at Daddy. The other one was tall and skinny who was talking to Daddy.

"You remember Carlos Lopez, man?" The man asked Daddy as Dylan had a hard time understanding his heavily accented English.

"Yeah, I remember Carlos," Daddy said that sounded like he was mad at the man for asking.

"Well, we're Carlos' friends," the fat man told Daddy. Dylan noticed that Daddy saw something, and he saw a look of fear cross his face briefly. *What is Daddy looking at?*

Dylan and Mommy screamed when a flash of bright light erupted from inside the fat man's coat and startled by the boom-boom of loud firecracker sounds. Dylan felt himself wet his pants as he started crying. They then heard a loud thump against the front door and Mommy ran to the door and opened it.

"No!" Mommy screamed, and he saw her fall on top of Daddy. He had never seen Mommy cry like this and Dylan ran to where Mommy laid on top of Daddy. *Something is wrong with Daddy. He is not moving.*

"DADDY!" Dylan screamed. He then saw the blood on Daddy's shirt; he learned what it meant, the sewn-on Seven-

Eleven logo on the front of his shirt, is where Daddy worked and where he would bring home Slurpies.

"DADDY!" Four-year-old Dylan screamed over and over again as he watched Mommy crying over Daddy.

Done with their job, the two men walked leisurely back to their Monte Carlo, started up the car, and drove away. They had no worries that the woman would be a credible witness. Plus, the orders were clear; Dave Baker was the only target.

The fat one drove as the skinny one saw the new young widow crying into her dead husband and the four-year-old boy screamed out in terror and anguish at his father. The skinny man whistled a sad Mexican ballad, as the fat man turned onto Van Giessen while the scene disappeared from their mirrors.

Mark's Bounty

Mark made it a point to attend his friend's funeral. The funeral home stunk of lilies and roses from well-meaning mourners. *Dave hated these flowers. He preferred the pungent aroma of good Indica or Thai bud to these flowers.* Mark wondered whom these flowers were really for. *Not for Dave, he hated these weeds that stupid people grow and cultivate and cut to put in vases of water to watch them die.* Mark sat in the back pew of the chapel inside the funeral home and watched closely the veiled curtain where the family members sat.

Nicole told him it was a pair of Mexicans that showed up in a Black Monte Carlo with tinted windows. *I will find them, and kill them for you Dave*, Mark promised the casket that bore his embalmed body, dressed in a suit. *Will they open the lid for us to say our final goodbye?* It didn't much matter to Mark. *It most likely didn't matter to Dave if people stared at his dead person one last time.*

The chaplain said an opening prayer and his sister came up to speak about how great Dave was. *They hardly said two words to one another for ten years that I knew of, and she prattles about how great he was,* Mark sneered at the young blonde woman. *You didn't know him, you self-*

important bitch. The only thing you knew was how to make him feel miserable. A Country song? Dave hated country music! I'm sure he didn't want that played for his funeral. Who the hell put this charade together? Probably his sister, the bitch, Mark fumed under his breath. Finally, the chaplain came up and asked if anyone wanted to come up and say a few words for Dave and his family.

Mark walked slowly up to the front for everyone could see him make the statement he wanted to make, dressed in his signature double-breasted suit with paisley tie and fedora held tight to his head. He stopped briefly at Dave's casket, a varnished white pine and quietly prayed, "God, help me find my friend's killers," and then he stepped up to the podium.

"Yeah, if you don't know me, I'm Mark and I am a bounty hunter. The chicken shit that did this to my bro will get his, with this pointed at his fuckin' head!" He pulled out his Smith & Wesson.357 Magnum revolver from his shoulder holster and held it up high for all in the chapel to see. "That, my friends, is a promise." He holstered the firearm and walked out the chapel and the funeral home.

His pager went off as he quickly read the pager's number that flashed repeatedly on the small screen and fished out a Marlboro from his pack just inside the breast pocket of his charcoal gray suit jacket. Mark wished he did not have to have this stupid piece of electronic gadgetry; he felt like a slave to it, as well as the cumbersome cell phone he possessed.

He recognized the number as Pasco's newly appointed Chief of Police, Tracey Dickerson. He pulled out the cell and dialed the number, as he lit his cigarette and inhaled deeply. After the third ring, he heard Dickerson come on, "Chief Dickerson, how may I help you?"

"Sir, my kitty is stuck in a tree," Mark replied sounding like an elderly woman as he exhaled the cigarette smoke into the atmosphere. "Can you bring someone over to get him down?"

"Who the hell is this?"

"Mark, Chief; sorry I couldn't help myself," he replied laughing and coughing at the same time. "What's up?"

"You're a real piece of work, Marteau," Chief Dickerson replied in his characteristic deadpan manner. "Are you done with the funeral?"

"As done as I want to be. I don't really feel like watching his burial in this heat. How hot is it today?"

"I heard it's around a hundred now. Can you meet me at my office? I have a bail jumper I want you to go after."

"Yeah, I need something to get my mind off this shit. I'll be there in thirty or so."

Mark heard him say goodbye before he disconnected the mobile phone and started up his baby. He climbed inside his car, a bright orange Plymouth Barracuda AAR; the last year Chrysler made them, and he loved it more than any woman in the world. It made a very audible 340 cubic inch, four-barrel rumble as he shifted the stock four speed tranny into reverse and pulled it out from a parking lot space and shifted it into first. He maneuvered out of the three or four hundred parked cars of varying vintage and stage of use waiting their turn to leave.

He drove up the newly opened interstate and drove her at a steady 80 miles per hour, though the speed limit signs showed 60. Mark knew that this time of day was shift change and no cop wanted to bother to pull someone over now for speeding. He put the cigarette out in the ashtray as he reached the city limits sign of Pasco.

It's also Fourth of July. No cop wants to be an asshole and pull someone for speeding. Another thing that pissed me off about Dave's sister; remembering this date as the day of my friend's funeral and burial. Used to be, it was about fireworks, picnics and spending time with friends and family; now it's about remembering my bro was buried this day!

When Mark arrived at the Pasco Police station, still located on Clark up the street from the Top Hat, where there was no shade and the sun felt more like a branding iron on his suit jacket, or if he had just taken it out from the dryer. It seemed a bit quiet in the main foyer for a change that caught Mark off guard. The desk sergeant glanced at him as he entered. "Mark, what brings you here?"

"Hey, Sergeant;" the Chief called me over. He apparently has a job for me. Mark knew this always chafed the desk sergeant, because it meant one less job for his boys. He had a large paunch and his hair had all but gone except for wisps of white that surrounded his shiny crown.

"Well, I'll see if he's around. Maybe I can find me a cop around here that ain't so busy to go get him for you," he announced in a bitter sarcastic tone. His face had turned crimson as he flew from his swivel chair and disappeared behind a secured door. "Go get the Chief out here, now," the old sergeant screamed at someone behind the security door.

The sergeant returned, and the Chief followed behind him. "Come on back here, Mark." The Chief smiled at him and shook his hand. "I'm sorry I couldn't make it to Dave's funeral. It was a waste that he died the way he did, and in front of his family too."

"Yeah, I'll miss him a lot too. So, you got a bail jumper huh?"

He led Mark into his office, still in the process of moving in, and closed the door behind them. "Yeah Mark. There is a possibility you may need to go into Mexico to get him. We arrested him for possession with intent to sell. Someone got him bailed out and he took off."

"Who is he?" Mark asked as he opened a note pad and stubby pencil out from his double-breasted suit. He remained standing among boxes of packed stuff that covered the floor and occupied the two available chairs that sat in front of the desk.

"Santiago Lopez Sanchez; I'm sure you heard of his arrest by our drug task force some three months ago."

"Yeah, I heard of him. Wasn't he listed as a member of a drug cartel?"

"He was, and how the judge granted this person bail is beyond me. He's either the number two or three man in an established cartel looking to smuggle black tar heroin from Mexico," the Chief replied as Mark noticed how much more pronounced the lines on Dickerson's face had become in ten years since he helped then Detective Dickerson find Old Joe's killer.

Now, it appeared to be vendetta time for the Lopez cartel; Mark wondered why they did not go after him too.

"I think I will need to take a road trip to Mexico then," Mark said.

"Is your passport all in order?"

"Yeah, it is. Wait, I don't need a passport in Mexico, do I?"

"I'm not sure," Tracy replied. "Bring it just in case; you'll have all your bases covered."

"I just need to go to my bank and pull it out of my safety deposit box, then."

"Good luck. I'll see you when you get back. It will be the normal reward, twelve thousand plus your gas, lodging, and expenses," the Chief said to Mark as he handed him the warrant. They shook each other's hands and Mark left the newly appointed chief to unpack more boxes stacked in the middle of the office.

Mark returned to Dave's house outside West Richland and saw the same beat-up looking cars parked about the street for as long as he could see and cursed these people; for now, he had to park several blocks away. The afternoon began drawing toward evening and he felt the heat drained him as he walked back to Dave's home where the wake seemed to be running its course from a tribute to just another excuse for people to get drunk and stupid.

He saw two men he didn't recognize squaring off in front of the house screaming obscenities at each other, while Dave's widow stood between them seemingly helpless to stop what would be sure to escalate into the inevitable.

"Come on you two, knock it off and go back inside before someone calls the police," Nicole pleaded.

"I ain't going anywhere until he apologizes for what he said in there," said a tall, bearded man with tattoos on his arms and neck, like he recently got out of prison.

"I didn't say a God damn thing that wasn't true," the other man replied as little spittle specks splattered noticeably on his opponent's cheek, his black hair and mustache looked overgrown and unkempt.

Mark arrived on the front lawn just as the one man started to reach back with his closed fists and hit the other drunk that rained spittle on him. "Okay you guys, time to go home," he called out and walked in between the two men, allowing Nicole the opportunity to get out of their way.

"Who the hell are you?" The spitter demanded belligerently.

"I'm the sober asshole that's going to kick both your asses if you don't get the hell off Nicole's yard," Mark grabbed both men by their shirt collars to emphasized he was bigger and stronger than both and could easily carry out the threat. "Now leave!"

"Sorry Nicole, we didn't mean anything," they said together.

"It's okay, Dan and Ron. Go ahead and go home," Nicole responded.

Mark watched the two men hug her and then went to their cars across the street and left.

"Thanks, Mark, for your help," Nicole said as he could see the sweat form on her brow and upper lip.

Mark felt a lump form in his throat as he tried very hard not to break down in front of these people he hardly knew. He remembered that night three days ago when she cried into his ear screaming that Dave had been shot. He raced to the hospital and showed up in time to see Dave's sister tell Nicole, "Don't you worry your pretty head about the arrangements; I'll handle my brother's affairs."

He used every ounce of self-control not to hit her. Nicole did not deserve to be treated like an outsider. She began treating her like an outcast, not that she was not used to it. Mark remembered Nicole's family was so set against them marrying, they refused to attend the wedding, and apparently, they were a no-show today too.

"It's okay honey. You're like a sister to me," Mark said to her. "I don't want you to go through any more than you need to. How much longer do you want these people here?"

"Well, I don't want to chase them out of here just because of those two. They're brothers after all, and always get into each other's faces over some nonsense."

"It's only going to get worse," Mark replied. "Let's nip this in the bud now and tell these people you need your rest." They walked inside the front door, amid cacophony that seemed to vibrate the very foundation of this double-wide mobile home.

"If you think you should," Nicole said. "I noticed you left in a bit of a hurry. Is there something going on?"

"Yeah, Chief Dickerson hired me to go after a bail jumper in Mexico."

"I had a feeling that's what it was," Nicole said as she watched Mark, who has been like a big brother to her and Dylan, clear his throat to announce:

"Yo, everyone! Hey!" Mark yelled out in a louder baritone, which was heard over everyone else's intoxicated voices. The place became quieter. "Now that I have your attention, Nicole is getting tired, and wants to thank you all for coming here, but she needs to rest and hopes you won't be offended if you could take the party somewhere else," Mark told the large group.

Mark heard the rumblings and grumblings coming from some of the poorer slobs that did not have money to go anywhere else. However, they all went away, hugging and kissing the widow as they went to their cars and drove away. Mark had in mind to leave too, but Nicole stopped him. "I have something to show you before you leave that Dave wanted you to have."

How would she know what Dave wanted me to have? "Okay, what's that?"

"Come with me and I'll show you," she persisted. Mark followed her through the cool house and into their bedroom. Then he thought he knew.

"No, I can't do that," he said with a hint of fear and uncertainty in his voice.

"It's okay, Mark, he told me after we got married that he wanted you to have this if anything should happen to him." She went to the closet and pulled out a black vinyl case filled with cassette tapes.

"This one here he said he especially wanted you to know about." Her hand trembled slightly as she fished out the cassette and handed it to him; it was The Eagles' "Hotel California."

"Thanks, yeah, I really liked that album. I thought it was their best effort," Mark stated, yet felt confused by her last statement.

"I had a dream the other night that Dave would show you that his killers are there."

It was Mark's turn to tremble openly. "No shit!" He exclaimed. "Thanks Nicole, I'll keep it in mind."

He went passed Dylan's room where he saw the young boy sound asleep. "Don't worry little man, I'll make things right for you," he promised him in a whispered tone.

Road Trip

Mark left five days later at 4am, heading south on the newly opened Interstate 82. He had in mind to listen to a tape from Heart; one of Dave's tapes from the briefcase sized cassette storage his wife handed him. *If I were a heartless son of a bitch, I probably would have no problem getting her into bed at this vulnerable time. But that's not me. I loved Dave like a brother, and Nicole is like a kid sister. The people at the wake, who didn't know me, probably figured I was either crazy or the biggest asshole in the history of humankind, but I could care less how they thought of me.*

He quickly searched for the cassette and found Heart's "Little Queen." He found the song that seemed appropriate for this trip that he knew would be long and arduous, "Barracuda." It unconsciously caused him to place his foot more firmly on the accelerator, which in turn moved the speedometer needle up slowly but steadily until his dream car cruised down the highway at over 100 miles per hour.

He didn't notice until he passed the weigh station at the Washington border and glanced at the speedometer, announced "Oh shit!" He quickly let up off the accelerator and watched the needle move down to a more allowable speed. The highway eventually merged on to Interstate 84 and he drove west to Portland.

Fuck, Dave, you know if you had never gotten involved in that shit from the very beginning, you'd probably still be alive. He suddenly felt anger at his recently dead friend.

"Fuckin' drugs! Fucking drug dealers and their goons who made my friend a widow of 32. How dare they rob my Godson of a chance at a normal life! Motherfuckers anyway!" He slammed on the steering wheel repeatedly while tears of rage fell down his cheeks.

He listened to Golden Earring's "Radar Love," as he reached the I-5 interchange and headed south. He maintained 80 miles per hour speed, not thinking about the consequences as he stayed on the inside lane. He left his headlights on throughout, flashing his high beams at slower vehicles hoping they would get the hint and move over to the center lane.

He briefly caught glimpses of the town and city skylines of Salem and Eugene and Medford. Then by noon, he drove through the California state line. He listened to Jefferson airplane's "Surrealistic Pillow" cassette as he drove through Sacramento. "I wonder how many drug dealer assholes live in this town?"

He had to get something to eat and found a restaurant right off the interchange of I-5 and State route 99. He read the Sacramento Bee and found all the local news to be no different from the news in Tri Cities. *It seemed like the same kind of people are trying to make a name for themselves, and the low life types are robbing and stealing to survive or get their next fix.*

He ate a burger and fries as he read the sports page. When he finished, he lit up a cigarette and received curious looks from the staff and the patrons. The waitress came by and told him, "I'm sorry sir but there's no smoking allowed inside the restaurant." He glared at her with contempt as he grounded out the cigarette on the restaurant's floor.

It became twilight time when he paid his bill and left a three-dollar tip with the smiling twenty something server. *How much longer before I reached LA?* He couldn't hazard a guess. He hoped the meal, which was not very filling, would be enough to keep him going until then. *Once I get there, I can catch up on some sleep before going into Mexico.*

He pulled himself back in his car and started up the engine, shifted into gear and continued the drive south on I-5. He listened to Credence Clear Water Revival and Doobie Brothers cassettes, along with a cassette from the Beatles' and the sound track from "Easy Rider." He maintained the same 80 miles per hour speed, though now cars were passing him as he stayed in the center lane.

The night came fast on him as he checked the time on his wristwatch and saw it was 10:30. State Route 152 and the town of Los Banos showed on a highway sign coming up on the next exit as five miles away and another sign showing Los Angeles as 200 more miles to go. *Three more hours then*, he said to himself.

The drive seemed endless to Mark. He almost gave up on it until he started playing Bob Segar's "Stranger in Town" cassette, and his favorite 'Hollywood Nights' song came on, he punched the accelerator and saw the needle strike 100 and he felt the car vibrating slightly as he continued to the city of angels.

He pulled into an Exxon and filled the tank, ignoring the fuel price of almost two fifty per gallon. He overheard the PA blasting Guns and Roses that pissed him off more. *Fuckin' noise is all that is. Real rock is what I've got in my car not that shit.*

He finished and went to the cashier and paid over thirty dollars for the fill up. He found the Doors cassette called "LA Woman" and placed that into the cassette and maxed out the volume to drown out the music on the PA. He pulled out from the gas station and got back onto the freeway.

He found a Motel 6 on the outskirts of LA and parked his 'Cuda in front of the motel's office. The man behind the desk seemed more interested in watching a porn video on the TV set than in Mark, who stood there at the check-in counter almost three minutes before he happened to look up and saw him.

"Sorry, dude; can I help you?" He looked barely eighteen and had greasy acne complexion that matched the long greasy hair he obviously hadn't washed in a while.

"Yeah, I'd like a room for the night." Mark looked at the kid with the same affection he would show a bum. "Here's my license and a credit card."

"Yes sir, I'll be right with you," he replied as he jumped up and took care of his newest guest.

Once in his room, he made a mental note to get the address for the US consulate in Tijuana. He undressed to his briefs and went to bed with the songs that played in his head. It took him a moment to wash the music away and he felt relaxed enough to fall asleep.

Meeting Hector Gonzales

He spent the better part of the morning trying to get hold of somebody that could give him the address for the US consulate in Tijuana. He gave up on the third try and decided to plug in his mobile phone. *I can call while driving down the freeway.* Mark pulled away from the Motel 6 at nine. The rush hour morning commute already had traffic crawling at a snail's pace. He thought that he would be moving along faster than this though. Now he became increasingly more impatient and frustrated by everyone who traveled on this freeway. He quite literally could see the fuel gauge needle move down as he witnessed the fuel waste occurring on this commute.

Mark chained smoked more from pure boredom and frustration, than needing to cure his addiction due to having to endure this endless traffic jam. The heavy traffic congestion continued forever; even after leaving Los Angeles and driving through San Diego; and even going to the Mexican/American border crossing. *Vacationers is what I have to deal with!*

He did get hold of the American consulate and the person at the other end, informed him with an over exuberant voice Mark normally associated with a telemarketer, said, "You would need to register with them and the consulate building is located at Citizen Services at Paseo de las Culturas s/n Mesa de Otay Delegación Centenario C.P. 22425."

"Where the hell is that?"

"It's actually very close to the check point, on the main route, about two or three blocks away. You'll find the American flag in front of a stucco building."

He hung up abruptly as he had to brake suddenly in front of cars that had unexpectedly stopped. "Goddamn it to hell; who let the retards and morons out of their cages?"

Traffic stood still for ten minutes before it slowly began moving at a snail's pace once again. The checkpoint came into view and the smiling American Border Patrol officer asked him whether his stay was business or pleasure. Mark pulled out his Sheriff's badge and the arrest warrant as he replied, "Purely business, I'm afraid."

"I'll need to see your driver's license then," the Border Agent replied.

"How about my passport?" He asked as he fished out his driver's license.

"You'll need to show that to those gentlemen down there at that check point. I hope you get your man, Mr. Marteau."

"Thanks," he replied as he left the American checkpoint and greeted the Mexican Security at their checkpoint. There, he repeated the same process, but it took a bit longer before they allowed him to pass. The American consulate appeared rather quickly, just as the man said it would earlier.

The lawn and trees appeared well manicured and the adobe style structure appeared well maintained and clean. He parked his car in front of the entrance and walked inside the air-conditioned building offering a stark contrast to the heat of early afternoon.

A woman in her late thirties with a blonde wig smiled broadly at him as he came up to her. "You must be Mark Marteau," she said offering her delicate looking hand to him. He grasped it gently and held it briefly before disengaging. "My name is Marie Silva and I'll be your point of contact from here on out. This is Hector Gonzales; he'll be your guide and interpreter."

"I don't need no interpreter, and I ain't got no need for a guide. I'm no God damn tourist," Mark scowled at Marie and glared with contempt at Hector, a slight man with jet black hair.

Her smiled disappeared as fast as if he had slapped her face. "No, but you aren't going to leave this building and find whoever it is you're looking for without him. I know all about you Mr. Marteau."

"Oh, you do, do you?"

"Yes, I do. You seem to have this arrogance that you are always right, and the rest of the world is out to get you. Sorry, but this is the real world. No one is out to get you. The world could care less about you or your Don Quixote attitude. You don't know anything about Hector. Hector will protect you."

"No, this will protect me," Mark replied as he exposed his shoulder-holstered weapon to her.

Hector immediately yelled "Gun, Gun!" He went to a defensive posture, and pulled out a Beretta semi auto nine-millimeter from his holster and pointed it at Mark's head.

"You better think about your next move hombre," he stated in lowkey Spanish accented English that told Mark he learned this language in high school. But also, he meant business.

Mark slowly slid his jacket back over the exposed holster as four Marines scrambled into the room brandishing their .45 Colts as well. "Sorry, I didn't expect this."

"Yeah, well you better start," Hector said. "I don't have time to babysit a stupid gringo like you. I'll go back to mowing the lawn or planting flowers or spreading fertilizer."

"You're the lawn care guy? You got me hooked up with a lawn care guy?"

"That's just what he does when there are no other assignments. Budget cuts have made it so. I also maintain the consulate inside here because we don't have housekeeping service available," Marie replied.

"Fine, but I want to make sure he'll be part of the solution and not part of the problem," Mark stated to her, all but ignoring the twenty-two-year-old man standing next to him.

"You just keep yourself out of trouble or I'll make fertilizer out of you, amigo," Hector pointed out.

"Go get in my car before I change my damn mind," Mark replied.

"I have some papers for you to sign first, plus I'll need to convert US currency to Mexican."

"My money's not good enough here?"

"That's the problem Mr. Marteau, Americans get robbed and killed for American money. It's a lot safer for you if you're carrying Mexican Pesos."

He reluctantly unstrapped his money belt and handed it to her. She handed him the extradition papers he needed to sign and the receipt of money exchange after she counted out the bills.

"If you come back, we'll exchange the remainder of the money back to American dollars," she said in such a manner that set Mark on edge.

"What do you mean if?" Mark asked in a belligerent tone. "I have every intention of coming back. I still need to drop off your groundskeeper on the way."

"With an attitude like that, Mr. Marteau, the vultures will be feeding off your carcass within twenty-four hours."

He sneered at her as he turned around and walked out the door. Once he sat inside the car, he said to his new partner, as he pulled out a cigarette and held his Zippo lighter just before lighting it up, "I need two things before we leave this town; a good place to eat and a shitload of fire power. I'm not going to be buzzard meat without taking at least two asshole Mexicans down first."

"I know a couple of places, but you'll have to be out of the loop entirely. Okay?"

"Sure, whatever. Give me directions."

"You won't get two blocks and survive if you go; I'll have to drive."

"What the hell? I don't even let my mom drive this car. What makes you think I'm gonna let you drive my car? I don't even know you."

"You want the hardware; you better want to trust me to deliver for you."

"You're starting to sound like a commercial. Fine, but if you so much as scratch this thing, I'll feed you to the vultures." He pulled himself out of the car, lit his cigarette, and traded places with Hector, "Just pump the gas once and start it."

Hector felt the power and smiled as he shifted the Barracuda into first. "I always wanted a muscle car. This feels almost as good as sex."

"Yeah, well keep your dick in your pants and watch for cars," Mark replied to his new partner.

"Whatever you say, boss," he replied, as he pulled from the American consulate and headed into downtown Tijuana. "I have just one favor of you, amigo."

"Yeah, sure; what is it?"

"I have terrible allergies to tobacco smoke and become asthmatic. Could you not smoke while we are together?"

"Shit," Mark replied as he grounded out the cigarette and threw it out the passenger window.

Going to Todos Santos

Hector found a place for Mark to eat that specialized in American cuisine and left him there. Hector returned thirty minutes later just as Mark paid the tab.

"It's all taken care of," Hector said as he walked inside the restaurant. "We'll drive by my place, so I can pack a few things; then we'll go get your man," Hector stated in an assertive manner.

Hector's place looked like a slum house in East Pasco. It looked like it needed fresh paint and the yard looked barren and weed grown. Four kids played soccer while a young woman hung laundry out on the line. "Is that your family?" Mark asked in a curious manner.

"Yes, two of the boys are mine and the other two are from around the barrio. Do you have a family?"

"No, I doubt I'll ever get married. And I don't have time for kids," Mark replied, still watching the four boys pass the soccer ball around like he and his friends used to do with a hacky sack.

"That's too bad. Family is the future. Family makes everything complete. And family continues the legacy," Hector said as he proudly watched his sons play.

"Right now, I'm too busy running down bad guys and don't have time for the future."

Hector nodded as his kids noticed him pulling up alongside the weed infested yard, and came running, yelling "Papa, Papa." They admired the car and asked, "Sabia comprar Este auto?"

"No, no lo estoy manajando para Este hombre," Hector told his sons.

"Quien es el?" One of the boys asked.

"El estás Mark Marteau," Hector replied.

"What are you saying?" Mark demanded.

Hector laughed at the man's ignorance, and then said, "They asked about the car and I told them it was your car. They wanted to know who you are, and I told them your name."

Hector got out, went to his wife, and talked to her briefly. She immediately showed concern as he pointed at Mark, and then walked into the house. Ten minutes later, he came out wearing baggy brown pants, a long sleeve gray shirt and a wide brimmed hat to protect his eyes from the sun. He kissed his wife full on the lips that she returned and talked with him briefly, kissed him again and watched her husband walk toward the car.

Mark felt a twinge of jealousy at witnessing their act of adoration.

"Now, we go and find your bad guy, Mr. Marteau."

The highway seemed more like a mirage floating endlessly before them as they traveled south through the Baja California state. They seemed to make good time as Hector drove them toward their destination at a steady 75 miles per hour. Mark asked Hector about the hardware he procured from whomever. Hector looked at him briefly and pulled the Barracuda over.

"Come on back here to the trunk and I'll show you." They got out from the car together and walked to the trunk. Hector opened it with little fanfare and the displayed what Mark's money had purchased. Inside the trunk lay a pair of shotguns, four semi-automatic handguns, a sniper rifle with scope, two fully automatic sub machine guns that looked like Uzis and ammo for all of them.

Mark whistled pronouncedly. "I also modified your car somewhat. I had a friend hinge the back seat, so it would fold down, and we can pull out what we needed."

"Show me," Mark requested from the five-foot seven-inch Mexican.

He walked over to the passenger side door and pulled the front bucket seat forward, went to the back seat and pressed a release button to pull that seat forward on its hinges as well.

"It doesn't look like it would work very well if we're both in the front seat, though."

"Yeah, maybe you're right; it might work better if we just do half a seat rather than the full seat. The next town we go to, I'll see about getting it done better."

"How much further is Todos Santos?" Mark asked.

"Do you have a map? I can tell you," Hector stated to his partner.

"No, I don't believe I do," Mark replied as he went to the glove box and rifled through the contents to be certain. "I guess we'll need to get a map in the next town too."

They soon drove down the highway again. Mark realized what they needed to do was get to the nearest town, and then rest up for the final leg. A road sign came up ten miles, or 60 kilometers later, showing the next available town as San Quinton some 80 kilometers away. Mark watched the hot sun slowly settle into the Pacific Ocean as the day grew to a close. *We'll find a hotel in San Quinton and leave early in the morning.*

He watched Hector. *He can't be more than twenty; at least he looks that young. He still has peach fuzz for whiskers growing from his upper lip. His dark brown skin seemed to glow from the perspiration on his face. His sombrero, for lack of a better word, protected his brown eyes from the sun. But he does have kids that look like they're around six or younger.*

He watched Hector scratch an itch on his jaw line. Then he yawned noticeably as Mark noticed the speedometer read 65 miles per hour. He drove Mark's baby with a relaxed air; as if he has done this many times before. "Tell me about yourself, Hector."

"What is it that you want to know?"

"Hell, I don't know. You seemed to handle that Beretta like you know what you're doing. Were you in the military?"

"Yes, I was. I spent four years in the Marine Corp. So yes, I know how to handle weapons. You have no fear with me Mr. Marteau. I can take care of myself quite well. Who is this person that you are looking for?"

"His name is Santiago Lopez-Sanchez. Pasco Police arrested him for smuggling black tar heroin and our fine judge saw fit to grant him bail, and he promptly went back to Mexico. To add insult to injury, I've been told he hired a couple of guns to take out my friend, Dave. They shot him in front of his wife and kid. I would like nothing better than to just blow his shit away, but I was hired to bring him back to stand trial and, hopefully, he'll spend the rest of his life in prison."

An hour later, they arrived in San Quinton, a small fishing village that time seemed to have forgotten. It reminded Mark of some towns in rural Eastern Washington that seem to try to survive on a single industry and were just being lucky. *This town is like Mesa or Washtucna,* Mark said to himself. *If they get one bad year, the town will dry up and disappear.*

The town had a hotel that looked like it dated back to the late nineteenth century and a cantina that stood next to it. Across the main street appeared a church painted pink. *Or is it the color of the mud when it dries?* Mark looked at the other buildings to see if they were similar in that regard, and noticed they weren't. *Why would anyone paint their church pink?*

Down the street from the church stood a gas station with a mechanics shop where an elderly man bided his time watching the world sitting in a rocking chair and spitting chew on the concrete street.

Houses of varying degrees of charm and affluence ran two deep from the highway. Most were adobe and most had no glass in their windows. Unpainted doors looked weather beaten from coastal storms.

On the beach, gill nets strung out on posts to dry overnight so the fishermen could gather them for their boats and head out to sea in the morning. And the boats themselves, five in all, were capsized on the beach and their oars lay nearby or perched neatly over the bow. *It must be low tide,* Mark speculated as the ocean seemed miles away in the horizon.

Hector dropped Mark off at the hotel while he drove down to the gas station. He eagerly lit a cigarette, inhaled deeply, and released the acrid smoke. Mark's head spun on him as he quickly smoked the cigarette down before tossing the butt to the middle of the main street and walked to the ancient hotel.

Mark couldn't have known how intimidated he could be when he first stepped inside the hotel and an elderly woman greeted him with, "Buenos tardes, te gustaria una habitacion?"

Mark had no idea what the brown-skinned woman said to him, but he quickly assumed she asked him if he wanted a room.

"Si," he replied quickly.

"Oh Americano," she announced gleefully. Then she continued, "Es un placer tener a un Americano aquí."

Mark looked dumbfounded, bemused, and befuddled as he looked down at her and felt absolute terror bursting from his gut. *Why the hell didn't I learn Spanish in high school?* "Si."

She laughed merrily at him, and called out, "Pedro, date prisa y salir a hablar con este?" To someone in the back. A boy of twelve or maybe older came out from an alcove and smiled good-naturedly at Mark. "My grandmother takes great pleasure in punishing Americans when they come in and can't understand our language," he told Mark in fluent American English.

"Yeah, I felt that," Mark replied sheepishly. "As your grandmother correctly guessed, I need two rooms; One for myself and one for my partner who will be in momentarily when he returns from filling up my car."

The boy repeated everything to the elderly woman who opened the register on top of a counter, beckoned him closer and said, "Por favor, senor entra en el registro." He quickly filled out the register.

"How much?" Mark asked, as he opened one of the pouches on the money belt.

"Wait, Senor Marteau," Hector yelled from the doorway. Mark stopped, and Hector went to the elderly woman and spoke to her in a hushed tone, not that it mattered since Mark knew he didn't know Spanish. "You don't pay anything."

"But Hector, I get it all back when I get paid by the court," Mark replied with frustration.

"You can send us the bill when you get done."

"That's not how it works, but okay, I'll bill you when I'm done."

The elderly woman handed each a key and closed the registry before retiring back in the alcove from where she came. "You got us separate rooms?"

"I don't sleep with other men. Sorry, but I don't fly that plane or row that boat."

"I'm thinking from a security point of view. There is strength in numbers and if we are in the same room, we won't be targeted by those bad guys."

"When we get to our destination, then I'll seriously consider it. Here, I'm not all that concerned about the bad guys. No one is supposed to know what's going on but a very select few," Mark pointed out.

They went to their separate rooms and stayed there throughout the night. Mark had trouble sleeping though. He awoke from dreams that seemingly had no rhyme or reason to them. He kept seeing a fat man and a skinny man smiling at him from across a table as if they shared a secret or a common bond.

In another dream, tarot cards were dealt on the table before him and two cards kept coming up three times: two death cards and an eternal love card. He never read anything into dreams anyway. He never really liked to dream.

He felt blessed that he chose to put them in separate rooms; Hector's snoring echoed off the paper-thin walls and woke him twice during the night. Moreover, it never really cooled down sufficiently to allow Mark a comfortable night's sleep. He tossed and turned.

A fat man smiling at me with gold teeth gleaming in the sun light what does it all mean? Goddamn dreams, they're all a pain in the ass.

The next morning, they drove on to La Paz. Mark felt amazed by the stark differences of the haves and the have-nots here. *Perhaps it's like this everywhere*, Mark thought as how many VW Bugs traveled on the highway also struck him. *It seemed like pestilence here. I know they're built here, but now; so many?*

Mark saw how, when they arrived in La Paz, the beautiful beach front hotels and condominiums and cabanas announced where well-to-do tourists vacationed. Further up from the Gulf of California, adobe houses of the well to do business owners, lawyers and doctors lived; while at the top of several hills overlooking the city, multi-colored tin roof shanty type huts and lean twos populated these summits pronouncing the working poor who catered to the tourists in their beach front hotels.

"Where are we going to next?" Hector asked Mark.

"Here," Mark replied as he placed the Eagles' "Hotel California" inside the cassette deck and the stanza off the keyboard spilled out from the speakers.

Dusk or twilight descended on them as they reached the outskirts of Todos Santos. Surprisingly to Mark, it appeared further inland than he assumed. Hotel California came into view from a bluff overlooking the town, where several palm trees stood guarding it from the storm. *It looked just like the album cover.* Mark felt a cold chill move slowly down his spine and he involuntarily shuddered.

Hotel California

Those lyrics that Henley wrote entered Mark's mind as he wondered if after checking out, he might be forced to return just as he and Hector walked up to the front desk agent.

"Buenas noches, senors," the smiling young man with short black hair and clean brown skin said to them as they approached the desk.

"Mi amigo y yo quisiera una habitacion," Hector said to the agent.

"I also would like a room," Mark told the young man.

He looked at Mark with confusion, and then realized that Mark did not understand Spanish, and replied with a smile, "Yes sir, I will be happy to accommodate you," he replied in fluent English.

"I already told him a room for my friend and me, Mr. Marteau," Hector whispered in his ear.

"Oh well, I knew that," Mark replied as his face flushed red with embarrassment.

"You are aware, that we are due for a storm within the next couple of hours?" The desk agent asked.

Both men looked surprised by this news bulletin. "Well, no we weren't aware of this," Mark replied. "My business here should be completed before that storm hits, though."

"I see. There is a room available just above the lobby that faces the patio. Would senors like that?"

"It would be more secure if we know who's coming," Hector whispered an aside to Mark. Mark nodded in agreement. "We'll take it then."

Hector signed the register and he casually read the other guests already registered and their rooms. "Gracias," Hector announced as he placed the pen on the desk and grabbed the bag, leaving the bellhop opened mouth.

"Don't you have any manners, Hector?" Mark demanded. "This young man here is paid to take our bags. I can't take you anywhere."

"Sorry, man I forgot," Hector replied sheepishly. He handed him the baggage, "Lo siento."

"Si, no hay problema," the teenage boy replied as he hefted the baggage and led the way to the elevator.

"Your man is here, registered in his own name; what an idiot," Hector whispered in Mark's ear.

"Thank you," Mark said to Hector, but meant for Dave, whose spirit, through his wife's dream, directed him here.

"Oh, you're welcome, amigo." He heard Hector's reply as they followed the bellhop off the elevator on down the hallway to the room that he unlocked and opened. He set the luggage, such as it was, on a luggage stand that stood in front of the king-sized bed in the middle of the room.

The bellhop opened the drapes, and the windows and Mark smelled the pungent aroma of jacarandas, Poinciana and tulipanes invaded the room. Mark tried to ignore the smell as Hector paid the boy a tip and he left the room.

"I think that I'm not the only one here with a problem understanding your language," Mark said pointing out the one large bed in the room. "Don't get me wrong, I like you, but not that much."

"Hey, it's all good. One of us can sleep, while the other watches over your prisoner."

"Hey, it's all good. I'm not planning to get my prisoner until I have a game plan figured out first. He probably has an entourage with him, looking for an excuse for getting into a gun fight with an American."

"This may be his last night here, Mark. He's here now and you may not get another opportunity like this."

"I'm not disagreeing with you, but I'm nothing if not cautious. I've been doing this job for a few years now and am successful because I haven't gone off half-cocked. I want to spend the night checking out every possible scenario before I make my arrest."

"That works for me, boss. Just let me know when you're ready to do this."

"Do me a favor; I know the kid meant well, but could you close the window, those flower smells really sicken me."

"That's fine. Some people like the smell of calijandra rising up from the air."

They were both hungry and went to the restaurant to eat. The captain arrived at their table; they were the only ones in the massive dining area that seemed more imposing by the candle lit tables offering the only light source. "Would senors like some wine?"

Mark remembered the lyrics as he replied, "I want a bottle of your domestic beer and tequila back."

He looked at Mark in confusion, as Hector translated for him. He nodded and went away. Mark spotted a hansom older woman with an entourage of young men following her to her table. The captain arrived with a flourish to get her drink order. The young men came across as effeminate, as they seemed to faun on her like she was royalty.

Mark received his drink and watched the strange woman carefully. She made eye contact with him and raised her wine glass filled with what he assumed was Champaign. He raised his glass of beer in salute. She seemed to beckon him over to her table with her brown eyes. "Excuse me Hector, but I'm going to talk to her."

"You be careful man. She looks like bad news," he replied with suspicion.

"I'll be fine," Mark said frustrated by the Mexican's behavior, as he slowly walked across the dance floor to her table. The closer he came to her, though the older and less attractive she appeared. *She must be a rich woman to have these guys wanting to faun on her like this*, Mark thought. "Hello, ma'am, I'm Mark Marteau and wanted to ask you a question about someone here."

"I know who you are, and I know who you are looking for," she replied in what Mark thought a foreign accent, not Spanish as her dark eyes bore into his very soul, which sent a chill down his spine. *Who are you?* He wanted to ask the woman.

"My name is Katrina, and I am a seer. You came here to find three men and they are all here. Come to my room later and I will tell you everything you need to know to make out of this place alive. You may go now."

He went to her room an hour later. Hector stayed behind to load the clips of the three hundred rounds of ammo he bought from his friend. She answered the door and her pretty friends were gone. "I was expecting you to come with your friend. You trust me that much?"

"No, but I'm not afraid of you either," Mark replied as he stepped inside her room and heard her close and lock the door behind them.

"You should be afraid of me, Senor Marteau. From this point on, you are in grave danger. One wrong move could mean your death."

"I'll take that into consideration," Mark replied.

"Come and sit here, and I will tell you everything." He sat on a chair in front of a table; a crystal ball sat on the center of the table. She held his hand in hers as those bewitching black eyes bore into him again. He felt obligated to look away, but also felt helpless to do anything but continue to stare through her soul.

Mark felt transported in her spell as he started seeing visions in her eyes. They were the same visions he saw in his restless sleep he has had in the past week since Dave's death.

Then Dave appeared to him; she spoke, and Dave's voice came from her mouth. "Mark, it is okay I'm here to help you. If you see me again, you failed and you're dead. Don't fail! Whatever you do, don't fail. I followed my killers here. They live here with the man that ordered my death. He's the same man that jumped bail, who you are looking to arrest and take back.

"You must kill these two first. One is skinny and tall. He wears a hat like yours. The other is fat and has two gold crowns that you can see when he smiles. You must kill these two first. Only then, can you successfully bring the man you want back to face justice."

She seemed to spasm as her grip on his hands tightened, then suddenly she released her grip and fell forward on the table. He didn't notice she wore a loose fitting, sheer negligee, until he saw her elderly looking breasts spill out from the bodice. He left the room immediately. *This is a good time to make my exit. Gross!*

He made it to the room and he knocked on the door. "Hector, let me in. It's me."

"Who's your mother?"

"You don't know my mother, asshole."

The door opened slightly, and Mark pushed his way in. "They're all here, just as I suspected."

"Well, yeah, I told you that when we registered."

"The two assassins who killed my friend are here too, is what I meant."

"Okay, well what is your plan?"

He sat on the bed and wanted to blurt out the séance he just came from. But he tempered his response with, "I think we need to go on the offensive here and take out the two assassins first, and then we are assured of safely getting him and getting home."

"You have to know; it won't be that easy. It's not just those two; it's an army of these guys with lots guns."

"As soon as we take those two out, we get the hell out too."

"Did you find out what the room number is?"

Mark didn't answer right away. The one thing he forgot to ask the woman happened to be the most important. He closed his eyes in frustration and it came to him as clearly as if he was standing in front of the door; 420. "It's room four twenty," he replied, silently thanking Dave again.

"Wait, you saw the register; you knew what room they're in."

"Oh yeah," Hector replied sheepishly. "Sorry man, I forgot." Then the lights went out as the winds blew in from the west.

They searched the darkened hallway, relying on the feel of the plastered walls to guide them as they could hear the wind howling outside while they passed shuttered windows. Earlier in the evening, when they checked in, it had been dead calm. Now that the storm had arrived, it reminded Mark of those windstorms years ago, growing up in West Richland, counting his blessings that he didn't have to go out in that shit.

They found the stairway and slowly made their way up to the fourth floor. *How the hell are we going to provide an element of surprise?* Mark thought to himself. Just then, the bellhop appeared slowly descending the stairway with the white beam of a flashlight guiding him. He cast the light onto their faces as he jumped back slightly. "Senors, you scared me. Can I help you to your rooms?"

"Yes, please take us to room 420," Mark replied.

He smiled broadly, as he replied to the guests, "I will do that most gladly, senors." He turned around and began back tracking up the stairway, when something clicked in his mind, he suddenly stopped in mid-flight and said, "But Senors, isn't your room is 201?"

Mark pushed his .357 magnum into the bellhop's ribs. "Just you keep going, and don't say a word until I tell you."

"Si, Senor," he reluctantly replied as he continued guiding them up the stairway to the fourth floor. He led them to the desired room. "This is 420," he said, hoping not to be an accomplice in whatever it was they had in mind.

"Ask them if everything is alright."

"Esta todo bien?" The bellhop asked through the door.

"Si, Moy bien," they heard the voice reply.

"Ask them if there is anything you can do for them."

"Puedo hacer aigo por ti?" The young Mexican persisted.

The unseen man on the other side of the door apparently tired of this game, as he demanded angrily, "Quien es Este?"

The door opened.

Mark pushed the bellhop aside as he fired the first round into the center of the black target and watched the silhouette drop down to the floor. Hector rushed into the room, crouching low, his Beretta out and safety off as he spotted the other man in the room sitting up in the bed as the lit candle enhanced his rotund feature. "Usted gilipollas," the large man screamed at the two assassins.

He fired his shotgun blindly in the darkened room, hoping at least one pellet would find its mark. But both men bent down, anticipating this as they both saw the man's face, his gold teeth reflecting the flash of his shotgun, and they returned fire into the man's body. They saw him fall back on his bed screaming out in pain, as the shotgun fell from his dying hands, landing on the floor next to the bed.

"Ask him where Santiago Lopez Sanchez is," he told Hector through the smell of cordite and the ringing in their ears.

"Donde esta él dormia?" Hector asked the dying man.

He pointed to closed door and replied, "El alli," he painfully gasped. Then the fat man stopped breathing.

They both rushed to the door, expecting him to be armed, Hector announced, "Santiago Lopez Sanchez, es la Policia. Entrega y salir con sus manos en alto."

"I told him to come out with his hands up," Hector said to Mark.

"Thanks, I gathered that," Mark replied as he heard a rustling in the other room.

"Okay, I'm coming out," he replied in heavily accented English, correctly assuming there was an American in the other room. The door slowly opened as he came out to face his accusers. He dropped his gun that he held with his thumb, to the floor.

He might have hoped the percussion of the gun hitting the floor would discharge a bullet into one of these men, but it didn't. Instead, Mark went to him and turned him around, slapping the cuffs onto his left wrist, and then his right, locking them tightly, and brought out the key to double lock it.

Hector and Mark both seemed to sigh in relief as they led him out the room and down the hallway. The bellhop stood petrified in place where Mark had pushed him. "You lead the way," Hector told the bellhop in Spanish. But the young bellhop appeared not to comprehend the words coming from Hector's mouth. "Passer!" He told him.

When they reached the second floor, Hector said, "Alto." The bellhop stopped, and they opened their room. Mark and Hector grabbed the unopened bags and loaded magazines and continued down the main floor outside. This time the man that staffed the front desk said, "You cannot leave!"

"We'll take our chances," Mark replied.

"But the hurricane is come! Please, Senors. Stay over the night and wait for the eye to pass," the watchman pleaded.

"Mark, he's making sense. It would be suicide for us to try and drive out now," Hector told him as he held the prisoner.

"Fine, we'll wait for the storm to blow over."

They cautiously walked back upstairs to their room with the prisoner leading the procession, when Mark heard something like a creak just behind him. Hector stopped too. "Go ahead and secure the prisoner; I'll see what's up," Mark whispered to his partner.

He nodded and continued to the room. Mark pulled his revolver from his shoulder holster and walked carefully back to where he thought he had heard the noise. He walked right into an opened butterfly knife, that pierced through the cloth of his shirt and stuck painfully into his abdomen, tearing muscle and lacerating flesh about three inches long.

The pain felt so intense; he dropped his revolver in reaction to the surprise attack. He felt his breath leave him as he searched the darkness for the culprit.

"You're a stupid American to bring a gun to a knife fight," the unseen assailant hissed painfully. He quickly pulled the knife out of Mark's gut and attempted to stab him a second time in the chest, but Mark seemingly recovered his senses enough to stomp his size thirteen double E wing tip onto his assailant's foot with so much force, he heard bones snapping like dried twigs.

"Ah, shit!" He screamed as Mark threw an uppercut into the Mexican's jaw, knocking him back forcefully against the opposite wall.

Mark went down to the floor to secure his pistol. He fortunately found it right away and pulled the revolver up just as the assailant came charging on him with the butterfly knife in front. A window, which had been shuttered up from the gust of the tropical storm, somehow managed to splinter in half, showing Mark Dave's assassin lunging toward him with the force and anger of an enraged bull. Mark saw the rapidly spreading blood stain from his upper gut.

Mark, momentarily thought to himself a second before he squeezed off a single round into his chest, *stupid fucking Mexican*. He died instantly; a grunt escaped his lips as he dropped to the floor.

Mark painfully pulled himself off the floor and just as painfully, tried to walk down the hallway to his room. Hector, fearing the worse, nearly ran Mark over trying to reach the place where he heard the fired shot. "What the fuck, Sherlock; are you trying to finish me off?" Mark reacted angrily to the near collision.

"Fuck, I'm sorry bro. I wasn't expecting to see you stumbling down the hallway. You're bleeding. Shit, man, you're hurt."

"Yeah, I guess we shouldn't have assumed they were both dead, because I got stabbed by that skinny fuck; nailed me really good too."

Hector shined the flashlight on the area of the wound, and he gasped, "Holy Mother of God."

"Go see if this place has any kind of first aid kit so I can somehow try and stop the bleeding."

"You got it man. I'll be right back," Hector replied as he ran down the hallway as the white beam led his way.

Mark slowly moved his way down the last twenty-five feet to his room where he immediately went into the bathroom. He carefully and painfully unbuttoned his shirt and wanted to scream as he tried to pull it off his torso. It felt like a fire had been started inside him. He grabbed two towels, placed them into the sink, and turned on the taps, silently praying the water hadn't been shut off, and thanking God that they were running as both towels became soaked and he placed both over the bleeding wound.

He applied as much pressure as his painful stomach could handle, while he waited for Hector. The prisoner laid on the bed, as he watched Mark apply first aid on himself. Hector and the concierge ran into the room carrying a satchel.

The night manager saw the gaping knife wound and reacted by turning his head and stated, "Dios mio." But then he opened the satchel, while Hector held a lantern over their heads, and pulled out rubbing alcohol, a curved needle with silk thread and a bottle of ointment. He poured the alcohol from the bottle onto the wound, splattering the strong-smelling liquid over Mark's stomach and down his trousers.

He opened the jar of ointment and smeared the greasy substance over the wound. He talked to Hector as if he was his father and Mark was but a child.

Hector nodded as he translated the information to Mark. "This is an herbal compound the natives use as a numbing agent like what the dentist gives you before he drills your teeth."

"Something like Novocain?" Mark asked as he felt instantly numbing of the wound area.

"Yeah, something like that. In a minute or so, you'll start feeling sleepy; go ahead and let the sleep take you; I'll be fine for a few hours, then we'll go."

"Don't you think we should be sitting on the bed," Mark asked, wincing from the pain.

"No, I don't want him to know how serious the wound is; he might see it as an opportunity to escape. You can sleep in here tonight, in the tub," Hector whispered in Mark's ear.

"That little thing?" Mark asked as he looked down at the cramped looking tub that couldn't be more than five feet long.

"You'll fit fine. El buen doctor will assist me in dragging your ass into the tub."

El buen doctor Mark thought about the words that they floated from Hector's lips while the buen doctor proceeded to sew the wound together, and his eyelids closed on him. Sleep took over.

Life in the Fast Lane

Mark felt someone shaking him awake. The first thing Mark noticed was that his back ached unbearably as he wondered how he ended up in this tub. The second thing, how eerily quiet it was, while he slowly put everything together. He saw he was completely nude, lying in a tub full of cold water. "Where are my clothes?" Mark asked Hector as the light of day filtered in from the room's east facing window.

"The concierge got you a new suit to replace the other," Hector replied. "But we got to go now. This place will be crawling with police, and unless you desire to spend the rest of the day explaining why two men lay dead inside this hotel, who may or may not be bought and paid for by Lopez or some other drug cartel, you might want to get dressed, so we can get our asses out of here."

"Point taken, thank you," Mark replied as he tried to move his legs and he painfully realized the wound was bandaged and sealed with cellophane wrap. "Fuck, that hurts," he cried out.

Finally, he gritted his teeth and willed himself out of the tub. Hector handed him a bath towel as he gingerly dried himself off. Hector placed his clothes on a hook-on top of the bathroom door and left Mark to get dressed in private.

The prisoner sat up on the bed as he watched Hector close the door, "What's wrong with your American friend?" He asked in Spanish.

"It won't matter now that we're going to be leaving; you'll learn more as we head north to Tijuana. Your body guard, or assassin, miraculously came back to life and stabbed my friend last night while we escorted you back to this room."

"That's what the gun shot came from," he nodded. "It's a long way to Tijuana; many things can happen between here and there."

"That's true, my friend; you might want to consider that if we get into a situation where we might need to decide to cut our losses."

"I understand."

"Very good; so long as we understand what is really at stake here, then there shouldn't be any problems."

"None that I can see, my friend," he replied just as Mark hobbled out from the bathroom, his face pinched in a grimace of pain.

"What's going on?" Mark asked.

"We were having a little heart to heart making sure we understand what's at stake here something should go down where a decision has to be made," Hector replied.

"Yeah, he dies, and I don't make my bounty. I had an expensive vacation instead. It would be to your advantage that your friends don't stop us from taking you back. I don't have to reiterate, that when the chips are down, you'll be the first casualty, not me or Hector."

"Yes, Hector said as much, though not as directly."

"Well, I'm nothing if not blunt and direct. You work with us, and I'll give the judge a good word. Maybe, he might reduce your sentence." He opened the revolver's cylinder, took out four shell casings, and replaced them with four fresh rounds. "Are we ready?" They both nodded, "let's go then."

As soon as they made their way to the lobby, two local police officers came into the hotel's entrance. "What do you want to do Mr. Marteau?" Hector asked as his hand made his way to the holster on his hip.

"Hey, I'm so glad you're here," Mark began. "This is my prisoner, and this is my guide from the US consulate in Tijuana. I am authorized by this arrest warrant here to take this man back to Pasco, Washington for violating his bail restrictions. Last night, his bodyguards tried to prevent me from carrying out my lawful duty as a deputy of the court, and I had to resort to deadly force. I am leaving now. Do you have any questions?"

Both officers looked from Mark to Hector, waiting for a translation, but Hector wasn't offering.

"Do you think they understood me, Hector?"

"Maybe the part about Tijuana; but, no not a word before or after that," Hector replied smiling at the officers.

"Okay, Santiago it's your turn to show how cooperative you're willing to be."

"Senors, por favor dejenos pasar." Santiago appealed to the two officers, "Me queria para el crimen en Estados Unidos."

"Are they buying it, Santiago?" Mark asked as he moved behind his prisoner, using him as a shield.

One of the officers spoke to them, "Como quieras." He added, "Sigue tu camino y que Dios te proteja." Both officers allowed them to pass. Mark and Hector led Santiago outside. They witnessed the devastating effects of last night's storm.

Debris strewn confetti-like all about the hotel's grounds, but fortunately no trees had fallen from the storm. Palm branches though covered the stone patio. The Barracuda looked dust covered and a few of the branches covered the car's hood, but no worse for wear.

"I want you in the front seat next to Hector. I'll sit in the back and watch for anyone coming up from behind."

"As you wish," Santiago replied as he watched Mark painfully climb into the back seat. Once he sat down, Hector helped Santiago sit in the front seat, and then went to the driver's side, pulling all the palm branches off the car before he sat down. The ignition engaged.

Hector released the clutch and the car slowly rumbled out from the patio moved down the narrow, winding Calle, then to the highway. He used the windshield wash button to push away the grime and muck from the windshield before shifting into higher gears. Soon they were on the highway heading toward La Paz. They could see the front moving north as Hector shifted the transmission to highway cruising speed.

They could see how much damage had occurred last night, but fortunately, the storm had not been strong enough to blow down trees or buildings. No one could relax though. It's as if they knew, the officers or someone would realize that a hole needed to be filled, or a death needed to be avenged before they could be free.

Mark felt the most uncomfortable, if for no other reason than his obvious pain from the stab wound. "How fast are you driving?"

"Around 70, boss," Hector replied looking up at Mark from the rear-view mirror.

Mark nodded as they skirted around La Paz and headed up the route they came yesterday. He tried to catch glimpses of the highway behind them, using the side view mirrors on either side of his car. He seemed to have a decent vantage point. Mark felt most surprised by the lack of traffic on the highway as they continued driving west on Highway 1.

Three hours later, the highway became more fluid as traffic became heavier while the day wore on. The divided highway had narrowed to two lanes and yet, all three occupants felt uncomfortable; one could cut the tension with a knife. They skirted pass Ciudad Insurgents.

Hector pulled next to a taco stand. He quickly went to the vendor and bought three plastic platters of tacos, rice and beans with three bottles of Dos X Beer. He handed them their platters and beers, along with forks. "Sorry man, but the beers were all that they offered to drink. You definitely don't want to drink the water out here," he told Mark. "I need to check in with my people. Could you hand me my satellite phone sitting in my garment bag?"

Mark handed him the bulky phone with the long antenna. "I take it my cell phone won't work out here."

"No, man not at this time; there aren't any cell towers down here yet. Take homage, though, this country will catch up with you soon enough."

"That's what I'm afraid of," Mark replied honestly.

Hector chose to ignore the comment, went out to the middle of the field behind the taco stand, and began dialing the number. Mark watched him talk animatedly on the huge phone. Hector closed the antenna rapidly and moved quickly back to the car. "We might have a problem. Those assassins that you killed were informants working for Mexican Federal Police."

"No, they weren't, they were hired hit men who killed my friend in West Richland."

"I don't know man, but the Federales are looking for us, along with whoever else wants to get in on the band wagon," Hector responded. "I called for a helicopter to rendezvous with us about a hundred miles from here."

"Is it true, Santiago? Are those your loyal guards that you sent to take out my friend Dave, or are they Federales agents?"

"I've known them both since we were childhood friends. There is no way that they are Mexican agents. Someone is lying to you," Santiago replied seriously.

"That's what I'm thinking too," Mark agreed. "Let's get the hell out of here. I'll start getting ready in case we start getting unwanted company." Hector put the phone next to him while he moved back onto the highway. Mark pushed the release button and pulled out the more lethal firepower from Hector's friend in Tijuana.

That's when he spotted a nylon satchel that felt heavy. "What the hell do you got here?"

"Did you find something?"

"Yeah, I found this pack thing and it's really heavy."

"Those are both fragmentation and incendiary grenades that we'll use in case we get into something we can't get out of."

"That's handy," Mark stated, sounding impressed by the forethought.

The car moved northeast and then north up the Gulf of California coast to Loreto. That's where they found trouble as a pair of black Suburban SUVs rolled up on them from seemingly out of nowhere. "We got company. Are they yours Santiago?"

"No man, they aren't mine. They could be Federales."

The first SUV passed them and headed up, while the other held back following from a forty-meter distance. "They're trying to block us in," Mark commented. "Punch it and pass the first one."

Hector did just that, feeling the three hundred horsepower engine kick in as he moved up to and then passed, the black Suburban. Mark rolled his window down and kept his Uzi sub-machinegun at the ready but hidden just enough for the passenger not to see. The Suburban's side windows were heavily tinted, so they couldn't see who was inside, or how many.

The driver's window rolled down and the agent showed his badge at the same time Mark pulled up the warrant, and his badge, to show him he had a legal duty to be here. But rather than acknowledge the warrant and letting them continue their way, the back window rolled down. Mark saw the shotgun come out from the window by way of the side view mirror.

"Brake hard!" Mark ordered so loud it startled Santiago.

Hector did, throwing all three men forward on their seats just as the shotgun blast fired in front of them, peppering the windshield with powder residue and the heavier buck shot rushed out the barrel and flew harmlessly into the desert.

The SUV behind them rushed past them as well, not having expected the car to brake. "Hand me that frag grenade, Mark." Hector commanded. "I want to even the odds a little bit."

Mark pulled the bag up to his lap and pulled out what he assumed was the grenade Hector wanted. Hector assumed Mark knew the difference and did not double check to make sure. He pulled the pin and popped the spoon, throwing it forward in front of the car; Hector then threw the shifter into reverse as the two SUVs finally stopped and turned around to pursue them, as Hector backed the Cuda up quickly to get out of range of the blast diameter.

There was no explosion though. Instead, the grenade puffed out smoke and fire as both SUVs drove over the burning object. "Shit man, you gave me the wrong one. It's green with a yellow stripe," Hector yelled at Mark.

"Damn, I'm sorry," Mark replied as he looked quickly in the bag and found the correct grenade and handed it up to Hector, who quickly glanced at it, pulled the pin, and popped the spoon, dropping it on the highway's cement pavement as he continued driving in reverse in the opposite lane. The lead SUV came up to the grenade.

At the same time, it bounced up to front-hood-level and exploded. Shrapnel cut the hood off turning it into a convertible and killing the driver and passenger instantly.

The vehicle continued forward without the control needed and turned abruptly right into the embankment.

Mark could see the occupants in the rear seat, bloodied and torn helplessly coming along for the ride as it flipped on its side, ejecting the two occupants. The blast's percussion jarred the Barracuda and Hector had a hard time maintaining control.

He braked hard again to keep the car on the pavement, while the second SUV came up on them too fast for them to react to this and slammed head-on into Mark's beloved Barracuda. Hector and Santiago somehow got out of this reasonably unscathed, but the two Mexican Federales in the front seat apparently didn't believe in safety belts and their heads slammed through the windshield glass.

Hector appeared briefly dazed, but recovered enough to extricate himself from the car, hissing and steaming hot water escaping from the twisted and mangled front grille.

Hector's nine-millimeter Berretta came out instantly as the two backseat riders came out, clearly shaken and without their wits or weapons. Hector shot both men dead. Mark heard helicopter blades approaching from the west.

Mark tried to pull himself from the car's driver side. He went to his prisoner and pulled the door open, the unmistakable sound of metal grinding against metal could be heard making Mark's stomach turn.

"Hurry up and get out. Next time I'll fly to wherever to get my man." Mark yelled while he watched the helicopter land realizing he will need to buy himself a new car. He only carried liability and was very certain his insurance was only good for the United States, not a foreign country. He and Santiago moved as quickly as possible to where the helicopter landed.

Then something made him stop, just as he heard a rifle report, and he could not for the life of him figure out why he could not go any further. He noticed the rapidly forming blood stain on his suit jacket and felt his ability to walk leave him, as he collapsed to the ground; he found it increasingly difficult to breathe.

Before he lost consciousness, Mark saw one man come from the brush where the first SUV had flipped, an M-16A1 in his bloodied hands, his face and exposed chest peppered grotesquely with metal and glass shrapnel. Hector ran up from behind him and finished him off with a nine-millimeter slug to his head.

Mark heard Santiago scream at Hector, "Come and help me get him," then Mark saw darkness.

He saw Dave and he figured he had failed. "Dave, I'm sorry I didn't get to finish the mission."

"Brother, you didn't fail. It's not your time. You still have many things left to accomplish yet. Go ahead, finish your work, and I'll be here waiting for you."

Mark felt a sudden pain in his chest, and another as he watched Dave's face fade away and he awoke in the hospital. He saw Hector and told him, "You owe me a car, you Mexican son of a bitch."

15 October 2014

Mark stopped at an intersection that announced US 2 on a big green sign, North to Kalispell and South to Missoula. He took a left turn and took the south route toward Missoula as he remembered a similar road trip that had taken them into the FBI.

END